WYOMING'S MOST ELIGIBLE BACHELORS

1. Chad Randall
2. Pete Randall
3. Brett Randall
4. <u>Jake Randall</u>

<u>Cons</u>	<u>Pros</u>
hard-hearted	good-lookin'
mule-headed	hot-blooded
love 'em & leave 'em	rough & ready

No contest—the Randall Brothers are the best catch in the county!

Their response: "Wild horses can't make us take a wife!"

Dear Reader,

Jake Randall stopped at nothing to get little brothers Chad, Pete and Brett married off and populating the Randall ranch with herds of little ones. Well, the tables get turned in this one, the last of my 4 BRIDES FOR 4 BROTHERS miniseries.

I love big families who care about each other, and I love cowboys. Out there on their Wyoming ranch, the Randall brothers fill both bills. As oldest brother and keeper of the family, Jake felt responsible for the fact that none of his brothers had married, so he set out to play Cupid for them. Like most big brothers, he thought he knew best. And like most younger brothers, Chad, Pete and Brett didn't cooperate. I hope their stories made you laugh out loud and made you want to join the Randalls in their pursuit of love.

I'm sorry to have to leave the ranch and say goodbye to the Randall brothers. They've been great company to me. I hope you've enjoyed their stories as much as I have.

Best wishes,

Judy Christenberry

Judy
Christenberry

COWBOY SURRENDER

Harlequin Books

TORONTO • NEW YORK • LONDON
AMSTERDAM • PARIS • SYDNEY • HAMBURG
STOCKHOLM • ATHENS • TOKYO • MILAN
MADRID • WARSAW • BUDAPEST • AUCKLAND

To Barbara Hunt, who, like Jake, feels responsible for the rest of us. No one could ask for a better sister.

ISBN 0-373-16665-6

COWBOY SURRENDER

Copyright © 1997 by Judy Christenberry.

Printed in U.S.A.

Prologue

"You need to sell your cows and replace them with ostriches."

Jake Randall's head jerked up, and he stared at the woman sitting to his left at the kitchen table. "I beg your pardon?"

"Ostriches are the latest thing. I'm sure you would do well with them. And you should paint your barns red. That's the color people expect to see."

Even as he spoke to his guest, Jake turned to glare at his sister-in-law Janie, seated halfway down the table. "I didn't realize you were an authority on ranching, Miss Quentin."

"Just a case of using common sense. I think the ranch would be more attractive if your employees wore uniforms, too. Maybe black pants and turquoise shirts."

Jake swallowed carefully before saying, "Thank you for the suggestion. Are you going to be in Wyoming long?" He hoped not.

Janie spoke before her friend could answer. "Allison is thinking of settling here."

"Oh, really," Jake sent a silent prayer upward that she chose another part of the vast state of Wyoming, far away from the Randall spread he and his brothers owned.

"It all depends," Allison Quentin murmured, suddenly batting her eyes at Jake. "I'm in Wyoming to find a husband. I've heard women are scarce out here."

Not that scarce.

"MR. RANDALL, I'm so glad you could join Megan and me for lunch," the blonde gushed, patting his arm with a soft hand capped with bright red talons that any self-respecting wolf would've been proud of.

"My pleasure, Miss Baker," he said politely, but he shot a look of frustration at Megan. His sister-in-law had asked him to accompany her shopping for a present for her husband, his brother Chad. She had neglected to mention a previous lunch engagement until a couple of minutes ago.

The blonde's statuesque figure was encased in a tight black dress, cut low to expose her charms. When she leaned toward him to talk, Jake had a fascinating picture in his mind of her popping out of the dress like a hot dog bursting from its skin when it was cooked.

"I'm thrilled to meet a real live cowboy," Mindy Baker cooed. Her hand traveled up and down his sleeve, as if seeking entrance to what lay below the fabric.

"You've never met Chad, Megan's husband?"

She giggled, her bosom shaking like gelatin. "Well, of course I have, silly, but he's married."

"Cowboys can't be married?"

"Of course they can, but I'm not interested in married cowboys." She batted her fake eyelashes at him.

Uh-oh. Not again!

JAKE LOOKED FORWARD to dinner with his family. His three brothers and their wives were pleasant company, and his new twin nephews were special delights.

Yeah, life was good.

He swung into the kitchen, a smile on his face, only to find his favorite room in the house empty, the table not set for dinner. What the hell…?

"Jake?" Red called, following him into the room. "We're eating in the dining room tonight."

A sense of foreboding filling him, Jake asked, "Why?"

The cowboy-turned-housekeeper walked directly to the oven, not even glancing at Jake. "We have company tonight, a friend of Anna's."

"An unmarried friend of Anna's?" Jake asked carefully.

"How would I know?" Red answered, again not meeting his gaze. "Come on, everyone else is ready to eat."

Jake followed Red into the formal dining room, but

he would've preferred retreating to his bedroom. He was beginning to feel hunted.

Anna, his newest sister-in-law, a petite, red-headed whirlwind, met him at the door. "Jake, I hope you don't mind, but I've invited one of my nursing professors from Casper to stay a few days with us. She's never been on a ranch before."

"It's your home, Anna. Of course you can invite your friends to stay."

"Janice, let me introduce you to Jake, Brett's brother. Jake, this is Janice Kobell."

"How do you do, Miss Kobell. It is 'Miss,' isn't it?" he asked a trifle grimly.

"Yes, it is, though, of course, I'm always hoping to find that special man. I can't tell you how frustrating and difficult it is to find any kind of man in the city. They're all so wimpy. That's why I decided to accept Anna's invitation. She assured me the Randall men would never be considered wimpy. And she was so right. You are a wonderful specimen, Jake. I can't wait to observe you in...action."

Her eyelashes blinked so furiously, Jake wondered if she had something in her eye.

"You're welcome to watch all of us work," he said, taking a step back.

Janice stepped closer to him, her nostrils flaring, as she reached out to stroke his chest. "Oh, Jake, I'm not talking about work."

Jake lost his appetite.

Chapter One

"Crazy women!" Jake Randall muttered as he charged into the barn.

There was a sharp wind blowing outside, foretelling the cold winter that would soon follow. But it was only October and Jake, a veteran of thirty-four previous Wyoming winters, hadn't been chased inside by the weather. No, his problem was women.

"Something wrong?" a cool feminine voice asked.

Jake spun around in surprise. He had supposed he was alone. Instead, he found himself facing B. J. Anderson, the local veterinarian who lived on his and his brothers' ranch.

"I didn't know you were here," he said abruptly, and stuck his hands deep in his back jean pockets.

B.J. rolled her eyes and turned her back on him, continuing her examination of the mare in the stall with her.

Jake studied her. She'd been around since the first of the year, arriving, with her young son and aunt, almost simultaneously with the influx of women to the Randall family.

Women he'd wanted for his brothers.

Women he now wanted to strangle.

It wasn't that he didn't love his new sisters-in-law—or the changes they'd brought to the Randall ranch. And he adored his twin nephews, born in July. But he needed some relief from their female scheming.

"B.J."

She'd finished her examination of the mare and was packing up her kit. "Mmm-hmm?"

She didn't sound interested in a conversation—or anything else—with him, he thought in irritation. Not that he could blame her. She was a damn good vet, in spite of being female. He'd doubted her abilities at first, but now he backed her one hundred percent…as a vet.

It was as a woman that he had problems with her. Something he hadn't exactly kept to himself.

She came out of the stall, her long legs encased in slim-fitting jeans. She was a tall woman, strong, lithe, but no one ever mistook her for a man. In fact, Jake was amazed, now that he thought about it, that she hadn't married since her arrival.

There was a shortage of women in Wyoming. Even ugly ones were snatched up. Not that anyone would ever call B. J. Anderson ugly. Not with her beautiful body and long dark hair, usually braided, her smooth, creamy complexion that urged a man to touch it, her—

"Did you want something, Jake, or were you just passing the time?" she finally asked, interrupting his thoughts.

He turned away from her, hoping to clear his mind of the strange thoughts suddenly running rampant. "I've got a problem."

"Only one? Then you're ahead of the rest of us." She started walking past him.

Desperate for someone to talk to, he reached out and caught her arm—and then dropped it. The awareness that filled him the minute he touched her was part of the problem he had with B. J. Anderson.

"Can you spare me a minute?" he asked.

She shrugged her shoulders and sat down on the bench that ran along the back wall of the barn.

Jake considered sitting beside her, then thought better of it. He paced across the aisle between the stalls several times.

"Jake, are you going to talk, or parade back and forth?"

"You're friends with the girls."

His abrupt statement didn't seem to faze B.J.

"Girls?"

"Janie, Megan and Anna."

"Your sisters-in-law? Yes, I think I can safely say they're my friends."

"So what are they up to?" He watched her, anxious to see if she would cover up what he suspected was going on.

Her eyebrows rose, but she didn't look away. The smooth perfection of her face was enhanced by the hazel eyes that dominated it. "About what?"

"Me."

Her gaze traveled slowly up and then down him, taking in every detail before returning to his face. "I haven't a clue as to what you're talking about." She leaned back against the wall, crossing her arms over her chest, and extended her boots, crossed at the ankles. The picture of ease.

He raised his hands to his hips and scowled at her. Any other woman would be running for cover about now. B.J. stared at him, not moving.

"Don't you?"

"No, I don't, and I don't have time for twenty questions." She stood and picked up her bag.

"It's Friday night. What's so important that you can't take a few minutes to chat?"

Her mouth hung open, showing her surprise, which pleased him for some odd reason.

"To chat?" she repeated, an underlying current of humor in her words.

"Yeah, to chat."

"Jake, I've been living a few yards from you for about nine months now. You have never 'chatted' once in all that time. You have spoken to me only when necessary, and even then you never smiled.

"Chatting involves smiling, friendliness, common interests—"

"We have common interests," he inserted sharply, glaring at her.

"Oh, yes, you own animals, and I work on them. You want to discuss the latest breeding information?"

"No! I want to discuss what my new family members are up to." He paced back and forth again before facing B.J. "Maybe I haven't been as friendly in the past as I should've been, but—"

She turned away from him and sat down again. "What do you want to know?"

He frowned at her, surprised by her behavior. In the past, in spite of his attitude, she'd always been unfailingly polite. "Do you really need to go?"

"No."

This time he joined her on the bench. "I think the girls are up to something."

She rolled those hazel eyes and leaned her head against the wall. "Like what? Are they teaching Red some new recipes? Putting flowers in your room, lace ruffles on your bed? What, Jake?"

"So you really don't know?"

"Jake Randall," she said, sitting up and blowing out a deep breath, "I have had a hell of a day. I will answer your questions if I can, but I won't play games. Get to the point."

"I think they're matchmaking."

He sat tensely in the silence that surrounded them, waiting for her response.

A low chuckle, throaty and sexy, drew his gaze to her face.

"How appropriate." With a smile on her lips, she stood and started out of the barn.

"Wait! B.J., is that what they're doing?" He wanted confirmation. He hated to accuse them if he was imagining things.

She turned around, one eyebrow slipping up.

He acknowledged again that she was one beautiful woman. Sexy as all get-out in jeans, a flannel shirt and denim jacket. Menswear that he'd like to peel off her, layer by layer, until she was all woman.

"How would I know, Jake?" Her smile widened. "But if they are…how appropriate," she repeated. Then she headed toward the barn door.

"What do you mean by that?" he asked as he got up to follow her.

"Don't act the innocent. Everyone in the county would know what I meant. You were the matchmaker for all three of your brothers' marriages. Why not turn the tables on you?"

"That's not true." Before she could object—and he could tell she was going to—he added, "Besides, it was for their own good. They're all happy now, aren't they?"

Surprising him, she leaned forward and patted his cheek. "And now it's your turn. You can be happy, too." Then she turned her back on him again.

He circled her and stood in front of the door. "Look, B.J., I'm not asking you to stop them. I'll deal with the problem. I just want to be sure that is the problem. I don't want to upset everyone for no reason.''

Sighing, she leaned against the wall. ''But how would I know, Jake? I haven't talked to any of them for several days.''

''I think they started their—their plan a week ago when that airhead from Kansas City visited Janie. The one who wanted me to sell the cows and buy ostriches.''

Laughter trembled on B.J.'s lips, and Jake's mouth went dry. For someone who didn't mix a lot with the opposite sex, she had very kissable lips, soft, full, generous.

''Did you agree? Are you trying to tell me I'm out of a job unless I bone up on ostrich anatomy?''

''Don't be silly,'' he growled.

''Well, it's the only thing that makes sense. Why would someone touting ostriches make you think Janie was matchmaking?''

''Because the woman then announced that she'd come to Wyoming to find a husband,'' he explained, a triumphant look on his face.

''Probably just a coincidence.''

''Then Megan took me to lunch after drafting me to help her pick out a saddle for Chad. And we were joined by a Marilyn Monroe wannabe, falling out of her dress. She informed me she was looking for un-married cowboys.''

B.J. frowned slightly, then shrugged her shoulders.

"Still think I'm imagining things? Tonight I come down for supper only to discover Anna has invited a friend, a *single* friend, to visit for a few days. She's looking for a man, preferably someone not too wimpy."

"And you think you're the only nonwimpy man around?" Her eyebrows arched again, and Jake blinked. He wished she wouldn't do that. It made him want to trace their path with kisses.

He shook his head. "No. But I think I'm the only unmarried nonwimpy man in my own house."

"There's Red," she offered, her smile widening.

"Not unless Miss Janice Kobell wants to go one-on-one with Mildred."

He'd shocked her. Jake realized B.J. had no idea what was going on under her very nose. Well, maybe not her nose because her aunt Mildred and Red were together at his house, not hers.

"What are you talking about?"

"Sorry, B.J. I didn't realize that information would come as a surprise."

"What information?"

"That Red and Mildred…hell, they're hot for each other."

Her cheeks flooded with color, drawing Jake's gaze. "Don't be ridiculous! Mildred has no interest in— She's never indicated— She's never married!"

"So her life is over? Or do you not think Red is good enough for her?" He was growing irritated by her attitude.

"That's not— Mildred can— I think you're making this story up."

"Ask Mildred. She may even deny it, but she'll blush from here to high heaven if she does."

B.J. walked away from the door, a frown on her face, pacing back and forth as he had earlier.

"You're serious about this?"

"Yeah."

She paced some more, giving him ample opportunity to admire her body. Something he didn't need.

"Could we get back to my problem?" he asked abruptly, determined to end their conversation before he got as hot and bothered as Red.

She spun around and stared at him. "What problem?"

"The matchmaking thing, damn it. Have the girls said anything to you?"

"No. I told you I haven't talked to them in several days."

He sighed. "And I told you they must've been planning this scheme for several weeks. Have they said anything to you about finding me a wife?"

"No. Nothing. Maybe they placed an ad for you in a lonely-hearts club magazine." She reached out for the door, but he put his hand against it, holding it shut.

"What, Jake?" she demanded, frustration in her voice.

Clearly his revelation about her aunt Mildred and Red had distracted her. But he had his own problems to deal with. "Could you ask them?"

"You mean, could I spy on my friends for you? No, I couldn't."

"You'd better rethink your decision."

"Why?"

"Because if they managed to get me married off, who would be their next target?"

A wary look filled her eyes. Slowly she said, "Why would they choose another target? Maybe they're only interested in marrying you off."

"I don't think so. Success goes to the head. They'll start thinking they're invincible, that they can play God. And the next unmarried person in their target range is you, B. J. Anderson. They'll start on you next."

"Then I'll just have to hope and pray that you hold out against them, won't I?" She tugged on the door again.

"You could help me."

"I won't spy on my friends."

"It's not spying. You could just ask them if that's what they're doing. A simple question." He was close enough now to smell her, an earthy scent that made him think of summer. He'd better end this conversation soon.

"And they would tell me the truth, Jake. Right after they asked me to give my word not to tell you. So what would my asking them accomplish?" He opened his mouth, but she spoke before he could. "No. Don't ask me to break a promise."

"But, B.J.—"

"No. I'm not going to help you out, Jake. You're on your own." This time when she tugged on the door, he let her open it.

Within seconds he was alone in the barn.

Time to think up a new plan.

Chapter Two

B.J. crossed the yard to the neat little house off to one side. Lights were burning in the windows, welcoming her as they always did.

What was she going to do about Mildred?

Every since Darrell, B.J.'s husband, had died, Mildred had been there for her and Toby. Her aunt had kept house and helped raise Toby from the time he was a year old.

The three of them had shared a good life.

Now Mildred was keeping part of her life a secret. And it had to be because she thought she didn't have a choice.

Damn Jake Randall's hide.

The man had been the one drawback in her move to Wyoming. He hadn't wanted her here. Even when he finally accepted her skills, he still hadn't wanted her here. She didn't know why. She just knew he didn't.

The rest of the Randalls had been delightful, making her feel a part of the community, even a part of their family, her and Mildred and Toby. She'd tried to accommodate Jake's aversion to her. She'd avoided him, and she'd tried to keep Toby out of his way.

Tonight had been different.

Because he wanted something.   She opened the door of the house, still undecided about what to say to Mildred. The thud of little feet took her mind off her problem. She opened her arms wide, dropping her kit as Toby rounded the corner of the hall.

"Mommy!" he called as he launched himself toward her.

"Toby!" she responded. It was a game they played each evening as she came in. He was already in his pajamas, reminding her that she was later than usual.

Spot, the dog Jake had given her son, stood at her feet, barking as she hugged Toby. Then Mildred came toward them.

"Land's sake, girl, were you planning on working all night? You haven't had your dinner yet. Toby, get down and let's take your mom to the kitchen and feed her."

"Okay! There's chocolate pie tonight. Mr. Red sent it home with Aunt Mildred."

"How kind of Red," B.J. said, watching Mildred. Sure enough, just as Jake predicted, even that mild comment had Mildred's cheeks pinkening.

With loving concern, the two most important people in her life settled her at the kitchen table. Toby, almost five years old, carried a plate of biscuits to the table and proudly set them in front of his mother. Mildred added a plate filled with delicious food.

"Well, did you have a good day today?" B.J. asked her son, putting off talking to Mildred.

"Yeah! I learned to write my name." In a flash, he was down from the table and out the kitchen door.

"I believe he's going to demonstrate his miraculous feat," Mildred said, her lips curving into a tolerant smile. "He only wrote it for us ten or twelve times."

"Is he getting in the way?" Several months ago, just before the birth of the twins, Jake had hired Mildred to help Red out with the housework. Each afternoon after preschool, Toby spent his time at the Randall house.

"Not at all. Red and the ladies love on him so much, it's a wonder he's not spoiled."

"Mildred—"

"Watch, Mommy!" Toby exclaimed, running back to the table, a crayon and paper clutched in his hands.

After several repetitions of his new talent, Toby allowed his mother to finish her dinner. Then she took him to bed and read him a story, as she always did.

When she closed the door behind her drowsy son, she returned to the kitchen to find it sparkling clean and no Mildred in sight.

She tracked her down to the living room, where Mildred was watching a favorite TV show. Patiently B.J. waited until the commercial break.

"Jake and I were talking—"

"You and Jake? That's something new, isn't it? Maybe he's gotten over whatever has kept him kind of standoffish," Mildred said with satisfaction. "Want more pie?" she asked, standing.

"No, I don't. And I don't want to discuss Jake."

"I always thought you had a problem with him as much as he had with you," Mildred said, a teasing light in her eyes. "Like maybe he was a bit too much man for you."

"Mildred! What are you saying?" B.J. thought she'd kept her reaction to the oldest Randall brother carefully hidden. She should've known Mildred would see through her.

"Nothing to be ashamed of. A woman can't help her reaction to a man. And Darrell's been gone almost four years now."

"Mildred, this has nothing to do with Jake Randall! Or me, except— It's about you. And Red."

The easy grin left Mildred's face. "What are you talking about?"

"I'm asking what's going on between you and Red."

"Nothing! Nothing at all. I work with him, that's all." In spite of her protests, Mildred's face filled with color. Just as Jake said.

"Mildred, there's nothing wrong with l-liking a man. Red's a true gentleman."

"He certainly is. But that don't change the fact that there's nothing going on." Mildred sat down abruptly, as if she could no longer stand.

B.J. licked her dry lips and wished she could choke Jake Randall. "All I want to say is Toby and I want you to be happy. There's no reason to—to hold back if you and Red—"

"How many times I gotta tell you, girl? There's no such thing going on. I'm an old woman!" Mildred, belying her words, jumped to her feet and ran from the room.

The television program started again, and B.J. stared at it blindly. If Jake was right and Mildred was lying, B.J. didn't want her aunt to give up a chance at love because of her and Toby.

What was she going to do about it?

Damn Jake Randall's hide.

JAKE MADE SURE he was out of the house before anyone reached the kitchen the next morning. It wouldn't be the first time he'd gone without breakfast. Since Janice had made a point of informing him that she was an early riser, he had no choice.

Last night, after he returned from his "chat" with B.J., Anna's friend had sat beside him and talked nonstop until he'd been able to excuse himself and go to bed.

Today he intended to make another effort to find out what was going on.

When his brothers joined him in the north pasture, they made several comments about him missing breakfast. Then Chad pulled a napkin out of his jean jacket. "Red was worried about you and sent these biscuits."

Jake grabbed them.

"So it wasn't lack of appetite that had you out early? Was it the boys' crying?" Pete asked, referring to his twins' nocturnal habits.

"Nah . That's music to my ears," Jake assured him.

"Unlike a certain lady's conversation?" Chad asked.

After a quick look at Brett's guilty face, Jake shrugged and said nothing.

Brett spoke up. "Sorry, Jake. I didn't know Anna's friend was such a chatterbox."

"I can put up with a little talk," Jake finally said, "but I'm beginning to think the girls are trying to marry me off."

Jake was convinced at once that none of his brothers suspected the same thing. It bothered him. Was he so conceited that he thought every woman was after him?

"Why do you think that, Jake?" Pete asked.

Jake enumerated the three encounters that had convinced him.

"I hadn't heard about the lunch," Chad said, frowning.

"Janie never said anything to me," Pete protested.

Brett just chuckled.

His brothers stared at him, Jake with a ferocious frown on his face.

"What? It's funny. I mean, it's poetic justice, isn't it? After all, that's what Jake did to us," Brett explained.

"I don't find it funny at all. And you sound like B.J.," Jake growled.

He realized what he'd said when his three brothers exchanged startled looks.

"You talked to B.J. about this?" Chad asked cautiously.

"Yeah. I figured the girls might have said something to her about their plans."

"And?" Chad persisted.

"And nothing. She refused to help me."

"That shouldn't be a big surprise," Pete drawled, wrapping his right leg around the saddle horn and resting his elbow on it. "The two of you haven't exactly been friendly."

Jake ignored Pete's comment. "Listen, I want each of you to tell your wife to leave well enough alone. We all know marriage isn't a good idea for me. Okay?"

Brett grinned at his oldest brother. "We may tell 'em, Jake, but that doesn't mean they'll do what we say."

"Just tell 'em!" Jake shouted, and rode off to chase a cow, leaving his three brothers behind.

"Do you think he's right?" Pete asked, watching Jake.

"Could be," Chad said, frowning. "And frankly I

wouldn't mind. I'd like Jake to be happy. But Megan's friend wasn't right for him at all."

"Neither was Janie's," Pete said.

"Well, Anna's friend sure isn't," Brett added. "The woman is driving me crazy. I can't imagine what she's doing to Jake, drooling all over him."

Pete swung his leg back down and slid his boot into the stirrup. "Okay. We'll each talk to our brides and see what we can find out." He nudged his horse and, as he set out in a gallop, called over his shoulder. "And maybe give them a few suggestions along the way about who might attract Jake."

IN THE NORMAL COURSE of work, B.J., who covered the entire county, didn't see Jake more than once or twice a month, unless her family received an invitation from the Randalls. So she was surprised to run into him at lunch.

"B.J.?" he called to her as she was about to get into her truck.

"Yes, Jake? You need something?"

"I just wondered if you'd thought over our conversation last night."

Yes, she had. She'd tossed and turned all night, wondering what to do about Mildred. "Yeah."

"Good. You willing to help me now?"

She frowned. Was the man still going on about the matchmaking? "No. I thought you were talking about Red and Mildred."

"Red and Mildred? There's nothing to do about those two. Unless you intend to object."

"Of course I don't intend to object. But Mildred won't even talk about it. I'm not sure you're on the right track here."

"Did she blush?" he asked, a grin on his face.

She wanted to smack him. Instead, she turned away. "Yeah."

"Well, there's your answer."

"Red's not trying to take advantage of her, is he?" she suddenly asked, squaring back around to face him.

"Take advantage of her? Come on, Anderson, that's even outdated for Mildred to say, much less you."

"I'm an old-fashioned girl. Is he?"

"No!" he returned, his good humor disappearing. "Red is as much a gentleman as I am."

"Some reassurance!" she muttered sarcastically.

"When have I ever been less than a gentleman to you?" Jake demanded, his pride seemingly hurt.

She shrugged her shoulders. "Forget it."

He clenched his jaw. "So, have you changed your mind about helping me?"

"No. I think you can protect yourself without me coming to your rescue."

Jake whipped off his hat and ran his hand through his thick hair. B.J. followed his movement, wishing she had the right to— She put her wanton thoughts out of her head.

"I'm not sure I can. Someone came to my room last night after I'd gone to bed."

"Someone? Didn't she introduce herself?"

She watched in amazement as Jake blushed.

"I had a chair under the doorknob. She couldn't get in."

"Maybe it was one of your brothers."

"I don't think so."

"My, my, my. Maybe you're right. Maybe these women are desperate for a husband," she teased, grinning at him.

He reached out and grabbed her arms. "You're not going to think this is so funny when they start in on you."

Her breath caught in her throat. She'd never been quite this close to Jake Randall before. His brown eyes held her gaze, and he moved closer still.

"Maybe you're looking for a husband. Is that the reason you're not worried?" he whispered.

"No. No, I'm not looking for a husband. But I don't have to start worrying until they take you down. So don't give in, Jake. Resist temptation."

"Those women don't tempt me," he muttered, and pulled her closer still until her body was pressed against his.

B.J. felt her mouth go dry as his hard muscles were imprinted on every inch of her. She needed to protest, to move away, to do something. Quickly.

"Hey, Jake!" a cowboy called from the steps of the bunkhouse. "You eatin' with us?"

"Yeah," Jake yelled back as he released B.J.

She took a step away from him, drawing a deep breath.

"See you around, Doc," he muttered, and walked away.

As B.J. watched his arrogant stride eat up the distance to the bunkhouse, she whispered, "Not if I see you first."

"SWEETHEART, I HEARD you took Jake to lunch the other day with a friend of yours. Was it Mindy?"

"Yes, it was. Jake didn't mind, did he?" Megan asked, turning innocent eyes on her husband.

"Um, well, he sort of got the idea you might be trying to marry him off." When she said nothing, he added, "And Mindy's just not his type."

"I know. Wouldn't it be awful if he fell for someone like her? It'd be Chloe all over again," she said with a shudder, naming Jake's ex-wife.

"Yeah," Chad agreed, but he watched his wife closely.

"JANIE, ARE YOU up to anything?"

Looking up from the baby bed where Nathan was having his diaper changed, Janie stared at her husband. "What are you talking about? Oh, honey, would you change Neal's diaper?"

Pete moved to the other bed. "Hey, there, little guy. Is that why you're fussin'?" He started the change but he didn't drop his questioning. "I asked if you were up to something. Jake's got a bee in his bonnet that you might be matchmaking.''

"What? Who would I match him with?''

"Allison.''

"Good heavens, Pete, she's not Jake's type. That would never do. Besides, she'd drive us all crazy in a minute.''

The grin she sent in his direction had Pete thinking of doing some matchmaking of his own, as soon as the boys were tucked in for their nap. Some matchmaking between him and his lovely wife. His favorite kind.

"UM, ANNA, could I speak to you alone?'' Brett whispered in his wife's ear after lunch.

With a smile that set him on fire, she took his hand and led him into the television room. "Yes, husband mine?''

His only answer was to cover her soft lips with his.

Several minutes later, her cheeks flushed and her hair in disarray, Anna pushed back from his embrace. "Was this what you wanted to talk to me about?''

He nibbled on her neck, wishing he could forget working this afternoon and carry his bride up the stairs. But that wouldn't be fair to everyone else. "No. Jake wants you to stop matchmaking.''

Anna's eyebrows soared. "What are you talking about?''

"Janice. And when is she leaving?''

Anna giggled. "Soon, I hope. I had no idea she

would set out after Jake like that. Wouldn't it be terrible if she caught him?"

Brett shuddered. "Yeah. I wouldn't mind if Jake married. Only I'd like him to marry someone nice. Someone who'd make him happy."

"Or someone he could make happy?"

"Whatever," he muttered, and returned his lips to hers. She was too distracting for any coherent conversation.

JAKE CONVINCED HIMSELF his brothers would take care of his problem. And when Janice left the next day, he felt confident everything was taken care of.

Until Friday night.

He came down from his shower to find the kitchen quiet. Warily he headed back toward the stairs, but before he could retreat, Pete and Janie met him.

"Hi, Jake. We're going to town tonight to celebrate Pete's new contract with the Cheyenne rodeo," Janie announced.

"Great . I'll keep an eye on the babies for you."

"Not necessary. We're taking the entire family. Mrs. Mott is coming in to watch the babies and Toby," Pete assured his brother.

"Toby?"

"Yes, B.J. and Mildred are going with us," Janie explained, smiling before she suddenly turned serious. "You don't mind, do you, Jake? Pete told me that you thought we were, uh, but—"

"Well, I am a little worried about Mildred," Jake

responded, trying to ease the awkward moment. After all, he had nothing to worry about with B.J. along. The woman would scarcely talk to him, much less think of him as husband material.

"I'll warn her to keep her hands off you," Janie agreed, laughing.

They divided into groups, six of them in the sedan they kept for family trips, and four of them in one of the pickups with a crew cab.

B.J., thrust into the back seat with Jake, leaned over and whispered, "If you're worried about them match-making me with you, don't. I'll keep my distance."

He breathed in her perfume, felt her warmth down one side of him and decided her keeping her distance would be a good idea.

He'd known all along why he'd avoided B. J. Anderson the past nine months. He just hadn't wanted to admit it to himself or anyone else. But he'd better face it now and prepare his defenses.

She disturbed him.

She made him entertain thoughts he shouldn't be having.

She made him want to throw her on a bed and fall on top of her so fast she couldn't get away, and make slow, mad love to her.

"Here we are," Pete called out as he parked the car in front of the steak house in Rawhide.

"I hope they've got a table big enough for all ten of us," Janie said as they piled out of the car.

"Uh, sweetheart, we'll need a table for eleven," Pete corrected.

They were joined by the others from the pickup and Megan said, "Better make that twelve."

"Wait a minute. What's going on?" Jake asked, the hairs on the back of his neck rising.

"Sorry, Jake, but Bill Morris called. He helped me get the contract, so I didn't think any of you would mind if he joined us." Pete looked directly at B.J. with a smile of apology.

Jake almost chuckled aloud as he noticed B.J.'s reaction, her hazel eyes widening in alarm. Bill was good with cows, but he left a lot to be desired in his social skills. Served B.J. right, after being so unsympathetic to his plight.

But he'd forgotten Megan's words.

"Hey, that works great," Megan said. "I ran into Ceci Holmes. When I told her we were celebrating Pete's contract, she asked to come along. I couldn't say no. This way, neither Jake nor B.J. will be by themselves. So...you don't mind, do you, Jake, B.J.?"

That suspicion that he'd almost quieted roared back, and Jake wasn't about to be a patsy a fourth time. Without looking at B.J., conveniently standing beside him, he said, "Sorry to disappoint you, but Ceci and Bill will have to console each other. B.J. and I are together tonight." Then he wrapped an arm around her shoulders and squeezed. "Right, sweetheart?"

Chapter Three

B.J. couldn't have been more on the spot if she'd been standing in the center of the arena of the National Rodeo, all eyes trained on her. She knew what Jake wanted her to say. And the picture of Bill Morris sitting next to her, trying to paw her under the table, as he'd done once before when she'd found herself beside him, weighed heavily in Jake's favor.

At least she knew he didn't have any interest in her.

She slid her arm around Jake's waist and leaned against him, finding her five-ten height fit perfectly against his six-four frame. "Jake's right. We're together." She felt a sigh of relief travel through his body, sending tingles through her own.

"Really?" Megan asked, her eyes big. "Then I guess Bill and Ceci can entertain each other."

"I guess so," Jake drawled, then to B.J.'s surprise, turned his head and kissed her.

It was a brief kiss, his lips just brushing hers, but it shot through her like an electrical charge. She was glad he still had his arm across her shoulders, otherwise, she might have fallen.

When she gathered herself together enough to look at the group, she discovered them all staring at her and Jake, bemusement on their faces.

Pete spoke up. "Well, let's go inside, shall we? I'm starving for one of those thick steaks."

There was general movement, but Jake held her back. When the others were several steps away, he whispered, "See? I told you they'd start on you next."

"They weren't matchmaking," she muttered, ducking her head, hoping he wouldn't notice her reaction to his warm breath skittering across her skin. "But I've dealt with Bill Morris before. I don't want him touching me."

Jake frowned and lifted her chin so she had to look at him. "He's bothered you?"

She shrugged, not wanting to tell tales out of school.

"B.J.?"

"He tried to paw me under the table."

"I'll take care of it," Jake growled, and started into the restaurant, his arm still around her.

"No, wait," she protested, forced to walk with him. "I didn't tell you that so you could do something to the man. I dealt with it. I told you so you'd understand why I went along with your—your lie."

"It's not a lie. We are together," he replied with a grin.

When they reached the tables the waitress indicated, they discovered Bill and Ceci already with the others. Bill immediately moved toward them.

Jake pulled B.J. along with him, rounding the table to whisper something to Pete. Pete took Janie's arm and moved her down a couple of chairs, leaving a place for Jake and B.J.

"B.J., how you doin'?" Bill asked, coming to stand beside her, leaning close to her.

Jake immediately pulled B.J. to his other side, putting his left arm around her and sticking out his right hand to Bill. "Hi, Bill. How you doing?"

"Fine. Looking forward to visiting with B.J. Pete said she'd be here this evening. I never see you, B.J. Every time I call, Mildred says you're busy."

"I've had a lot to do lately," she said, but didn't smile. She didn't want to give the man any encouragement.

"And I've taken up the rest of her time," Jake drawled. He let his arm slide from her shoulders to her waist and turned to pull her against him, and he kissed her again.

He was going to have to stop that, B.J. reasoned, because it left her dizzy. And wanting more. She'd have to remember to tell him when they were alone—no, not alone. She didn't need to be alone with Jake.

Ceci appeared beside Bill. "What's going on? Are you two an item? Is there going to be another Randall wedding?"

"No!" B.J. protested, but her voice was soft, hoarse.

"Who knows?" Jake replied heartily, his voice easily covering hers.

Was the man crazy? Ceci was a nonstop gossip. She'd be spreading rumors all over the county.

Before B.J. could protest again, Jake pulled out her chair. "I think the waitress is waiting to take our orders. There are a couple of chairs over there," he said, pointing out two places on the other side at the end of the table.

"Beside Red and Mildred," Ceci noted with a smile. "Don't they make the cutest couple? I was talking about those two the other day. Everyone's betting they'll marry. I swear, you Randalls are certainly marriage minded these days. What a change!"

Bill pulled the bubbling Ceci after him, but he was frowning in B.J.'s direction. Not that she cared. She owed the man nothing. But she was concerned about the impression Jake left.

"Don't you think you overdid it?" she whispered, leaning toward him so no one else could hear.

"Do you want that...man calling you?"

"You know I don't."

"Well, I took care of it."

"But, Jake, Ceci will tell everyone—"

"So no one will call. Is that going to bother you? You got a hot romance going?" His voice had sharpened, and he leaned closer.

She swallowed and turned away, reaching for the

glass of water the waitress had just placed in front of her. Not only should they avoiding kissing, but also they should keep a lot of space between them. No close quarters.

"Don't be silly," she finally managed to respond, mumbling into her napkin.

"So what does it matter?"

"I thought it mattered to you. I thought you didn't want to consider marriage."

"I'm not!" he said sharply, drawing everyone's gaze. He nodded and smiled, but B.J. could tell it took some effort. Without losing his smile, he muttered, "Don't get confused. I have no intention of marrying ever again. We're just pretending."

B.J. pasted on a smile, too, but she ordered, "Don't you dare insinuate I'm trying to trap you into marriage. I'm not the one who created this—this situation."

"Fine! " he snapped, his false smile still on his lips.

"Fine!" she returned, and picked up the menu.

JAKE COULDN'T ENJOY his steak because he knew what was coming next. And wondered if B.J. had thought about the dancing that would follow. Maybe dancing with him wouldn't bother her.

But it was going to be hell on his nerves.

He was only playing a role, of course. That's why he'd kissed her. Twice. Once to convince his family. And once to warn off Morris. He'd never particularly liked the man, but now he despised him. He'd have to warn Pete not to have much to do with him in the future.

He looked sideways at B.J., calmly eating and chatting with Janie, who sat on her other side. No sign of nerves there. Of course, B.J. could handle emergencies. She had to in her line of work.

His gaze encountered Bill's as he looked away from B.J. The man was glaring at him. With grim satisfaction, Jake put his arm along the back of B.J.'s chair, his fingertips caressing her shoulder. Bill smoldered.

B.J. turned to look at him, a question in her hazel eyes. "Did you want something?"

"No. Just making sure Bill gets the picture."

"I think you're getting carried away, Jake. I told you I took care of the situation."

"But he's been calling you, so you must not have done a thorough job."

"Then I'll handle it."

"You're not dancing with him."

"Jake," she said in irritation, "I am not one of your brothers. You can't order me around."

Amused by her indignation and fighting the urge to kiss those tempting lips again, he leaned closer. "No, but I'm with you tonight. You agreed. So you dance with me."

"So you're only going to dance with me? Do you realize how much you're limiting yourself?"

"Not much. You're the best-looking woman here.

Dancing with you won't exactly be a hardship.'' He gave her his best smile, one that had charmed many a woman.

His compliment received a glare before she turned back to talk to Janie.

"Jake?" Bill called from down the table.

"Yeah, Bill.''

"How long have you and B.J. been seeing each other? I hadn't heard she was taken.''

With his fingers still stroking her shoulder, he leaned back in his chair and drawled, "Long enough.''

"Not long," B.J. said immediately after. "We have a lot in common.''

"Yeah, we like to chat," Jake added, grinning wickedly at her, daring her to recall their earlier conversation.

She rolled her eyes at him and then returned to her meal.

"There's been so much happening around our place, it's hard for anyone to keep up," Janie said. "Or maybe I'm saying that because the twins keep me so busy. You're going to have to come visit, Ceci. I don't think you've seen them yet.''

"I intended to, though I'll have to admit I was a lot more enthusiastic before I realized Jake was taken. All us girls have been talking about it now being Jake's turn to marry." Ceci giggled and then added, "I guess you've been thinking the same thing, Jake.''

Red stood suddenly and raised his glass of iced tea. "A toast to Jake and B.J."

Jake almost choked. Maybe he had gone a little overboard. B.J. was right about gossip spreading fast. If he wasn't careful, he was going to be married to the woman before the end of the week. At least in the minds of his neighbors.

"Uh, thanks, Red, but I don't think we're to the toasting stage yet," Jake said after they all had put their glasses down.

"Then we should probably drink a toast to Red and Mildred," Ceci suggested.

Both Red and Mildred blushed a bright red, and Jake hastily intervened. "I think that's enough toasting for now. I hear the music warming up. Let's do a little dancing before it gets crowded."

Red and Mildred responded to his suggestion with enthusiasm, probably glad to get away from Ceci and her ideas. Jake noticed B.J. watching Mildred. He guessed Mildred was going to get a few questions from B.J. later.

Grinning, he decided the next time B.J. thought he was bossing around his brothers, he'd remind her of her interest in Mildred's activities. Maybe he'd been more accurate than he thought when he'd said he and B.J. had a lot in common. They both tried to take care of their families.

They all rose and moved in the general direction of the dance floor. He rested his hand on the small of B.J.'s back, guiding her, but his touch became more possessive on her waist as Bill waded through the crowd.

"B.J., how about a dance?" he asked as he reached them.

"Sorry, Bill," Jake replied before B.J. could. "I've staked my claim on all her dances this evening."

"What's wrong, Randall? Afraid of a little competition?" the other man snarled.

"Not any you can offer," Jake said softly, fighting to hold on to his temper.

As if aware of the tension, Pete turned back and put a hand on Jake's shoulder. "Any problem?"

"No, I don't think so," Jake assured him, but he continued to stare at Bill. "Is there, Bill?"

"No, no problem...yet."

Jake smiled at his brother, grabbed B.J.'s hand and led her to the dance floor. With perfect timing, the music started and he swung her into his arms.

Tonight she was dressed in a soft denim skirt, with a blue-green blouse that made her eyes sparkle. Feminine clothes that made her more attractive, if that were possible, than her blue jeans.

"Why haven't you dated?" he asked abruptly.

She looked up. "Why are you asking?"

"I hadn't thought about it until the other night."

Her lips twisted in a half smile. "I know. You've basically ignored me for the past nine months."

"With good reason," he muttered and then wished he hadn't spoken.

"What good reason?"

"I didn't figure I had any business with you."

He thought he'd come up with a good substitute for the truth—that he was too attracted to her for his own good. Her response smashed that idea.

"And you have business with me now?"

"Yup. We're together. Remember?"

"Mmm."

They danced in silence as he became more and more aware of her. His embrace grew closer, and she surprised him by laying her head on his shoulder. He glanced down to discover her dark lashes resting on her soft cheeks.

"So you're not going to tell me?" he whispered, his cheek touching her silky dark hair. It wasn't braided tonight, but she'd pulled it back with combs. He wanted to take them out and run his fingers through it.

She didn't answer, only shaking her head against his chin. He smiled and closed his eyes, too. This closeness was too nice to waste. He hadn't enjoyed a woman as he was enjoying B.J. in a long time. Or maybe never.

RED AND MILDRED CIRCLED the dance floor, not talking.

Finally Red said, "I don't think you're going to have to tell her now. Ceci made things pretty clear."

"I don't know."

"Millie, I don't want to wait." He tightened his

hold on her, even though he knew she would protest. She wanted everything circumspect.

"Red, I can't just leave her and Toby. They need me."

"Leave her? You'd only be moving a few yards away. You'd still be there for both of them." They'd had this argument for several weeks now, ever since he'd gotten up enough nerve to tell Mildred how he felt about her.

It hadn't been easy. He'd never proposed to a woman before. And the hardest part was that he understood her feelings about B.J. and Toby. After all, he'd been there for the Randall brothers for as long as he could remember. Even now he wouldn't be able to walk away.

But he wasn't asking that of Mildred.

"You could ask her, see what she says," he pleaded.

Mildred looked up at him, her hazel eyes quite like her niece's. "I've been thinking."

To Red's surprise, her cheeks were bright red.

"What have you been thinking?"

"Maybe—maybe we should..." She sighed.

"Should what?"

"Have sex instead of marryin'."

Red came to an abrupt halt, throwing off several couples around them. He made his apologies and then led Mildred from the floor. At the table, he pulled out her seat.

"Mildred, if you're ashamed of me, just say so.

But I'm too old to sneak around. I want you, but I want you forever, not in the laundry room when everyone is gone."

With those words, he sat down beside her and crossed his arms over his chest.

Twelve times twelve is one hundred forty-four. Twelve times eleven is—

No use. For the past ten minutes, Jake had run through the multiplication tables to help keep his mind off how close. B.J. was, how soft she felt. But even the twelves weren't enough. He simply gave up and took her back to the table.

She paused when she discovered Red and Mildred sitting down, not speaking to each other.

"Is everything all right?" she asked her aunt.

"Of course. You two dance together real well."

"Nope. It's not all right," Red retorted.

"Red, if you say anything, I'll never forgive you." Tears pooled in Mildred's eyes.

B.J. left Jake's side and hurried around the table. "Let's go powder our noses."

Jake watched the two of them cross the room before he turned back to Red. "Anything I can help you with?"

"Jake, I want to marry her. It won't stop me from doin' my job. You okay with that?"

"Of course I am, Red," Jake said, grinning. "Congratulations, you old geezer!"

"No need to congratulate me," Red said, his expression glum. "The woman won't say yes."

"You've asked her?"

"Yup. But she insists she can't leave B.J. and Toby."

"Hell, you're not moving to Alaska, are you?"

"That's what I told her." Several of the rest of the family began to drift to the table. "Walk outside with me."

Jake couldn't refuse to follow the older man. After all Red had done for their family, the Randalls owed him their complete support.

Jake listened to Red for several minutes, commiserating where appropriate, advising where he could. Not that Jake was an expert on how to deal with women. But just being there for him seemed to ease Red's tension.

When Jake led him back inside, he hoped B.J. talked some sense into Mildred in the ladies' room. The music was playing again, but he ignored the dancers and headed for their table.

Megan and Chad were sitting there, Megan's head on her husband's shoulder.

"Tired, Megan? Do you want to go home?" Jake asked, concerned about her and the baby she was carrying.

"Soon. But everyone's having such a good time."

"Yeah. Have B.J. and her aunt come back?"

"Oh, yes. She's dancing. So is Mildred."

Both Red and Jake spun around to stare at the danc-

ers. It didn't take Jake long to find B.J. She was dancing with Bill Morris. He had his hand clamped on
her, and even from where he stood, Jake could tell
they were in a tug-of-war.

B.J. certainly didn't have her head on the man's
shoulder, he realized with satisfaction. With a sure
stride and a lot of determination, Jake crossed the
dance floor.

"Take your hands off her, Bill," he announced
calmly.

"She agreed to dance with me," the other man
insisted, turning a triumphant glare on Jake.

"But she's not enjoying it."

"No, I'm not," B.J. said, and broke Bill's hold. "I
wanted to be polite, Bill, but you're making it
impossible."

"Hey, I'm just dancing."

"No. You're holding me too close. I told you."
B.J. started to walk away, but Bill reached out to grab
her arm.

"I want to finish the dance."

"I don't."

"Turn her loose," Jake ordered.

"Jake, I'll handle this." B.J. said, turning to face
him. "Stay out of it."

"You're with me. I protect my own."

"I take care of myself. I don't need a man to protect me."

"Sweetheart, it's my right if you're with me."

"You're not listening to me, Jake," B.J. insisted.

"Hey, what happened to me? Argue with me, B.J., not Jake." Bill seemed affronted by them ignoring him.

Jake grinned at the man's distress. He guessed it was pretty sad to be ignored by the woman you'd set your sights on. He reached out to grasp B.J.'s arms. "Sweetheart, I'm listening. But you've got to understand how things work around here. If you're with me, then I take care of you."

"Great! Then I won't be with you, because I don't need a macho man throwing his weight around."

"Too late," he muttered, and it was. He'd watched those soft pink lips for too long without tasting them again. Besides, he wanted everyone to know she was his.

For tonight only, of course.

As a pretense, of course.

In the center of the dance floor, he pulled her into his arms and kissed the living daylights out of her.

Poor Bill Morris just stood there and watched.

Out of sheer panic, B.J. ripped herself out of Jake's embrace and swung her fist. She realized she'd made a mistake too late. Her knuckles had already connected with his jaw. And Jake stood there, his hand on his mouth and shock on his face.

Chapter Four

"Lady, you pack a mean punch," Jake drawled after the shock wore off.

Chad came up behind her and put his arm around her shoulders, startling her.

"Need any help, B.J.? We Randalls have had a few fights around here, but none of them with a woman. I don't want people to get the wrong idea." He grinned at his brother.

"Watch out, little brother. You're choosing the wrong side."

"Aw, Jake, you know it wouldn't be a fair fight. I've got to go for the underdog."

"She'd still be the underdog with you on her side," Jake returned, a rueful grin on his face.

The music started again, and B.J. turned toward the table where Megan was waiting. All she wanted to do was return to the table and hide. But there in her path was Bill Morris.

He sported a tentative look on his face as he started, " B.J., I'm—"

B.J. shot him a glacial stare that stopped him cold. "You'll be the next one with a bruised jaw if you ever touch me again."

Bill hurriedly moved away and B.J. walked on. When someone caught her arm, she whirled around, ready to do battle again, only to discover Jake.

"What do you want?" she asked, her cheeks red, sure everyone was watching them.

"A dance."

She stared at him, confused.

Without waiting for an answer, he pulled her into his arms. "If we don't make up, everyone will be gossiping about us for weeks," he whispered in her ear.

She heard his words, but her body couldn't respond to his warm embrace. He pulled her closer, forcing her to move her feet. "Relax, B.J. Everyone's watching."

It didn't take but a second to verify his warning. With a shuddering breath, she gave in to his persuasion and moved to the music.

After several minutes, he whispered, "Why did you hit me? I kissed you earlier, and you didn't seem upset."

"Not like that," she replied, her voice sharper than she intended. His earlier kisses had been mere brushes of their lips, not a soul-searching invasion. She didn't want to explain that she'd panicked. That she'd never been kissed like that, even by her husband. That she'd been ever so close to forgetting anything and everything but Jake Randall. No, she couldn't explain those things to Jake.

He pulled his head back to stare down at her.

She determinedly looked away. Holding her breath, afraid he'd ask more questions she didn't want to answer, she tried to follow his lead but hold her body apart from his.

"Relax." His order was delivered in a soft voice, but she recognized a note of inflexibility in it.

With a deep breath, she tried to resist, but his warm body was tempting, inviting. He pulled her closer, giving her no option about the distance between them. Then he dropped her right hand and linked his hands behind her back. Without conscious thought, her hand joined with the other behind his neck, and they danced slowly about the room, pressed one against the other.

As the music ended, awakening her from the dreamy state she'd been in, Jake whispered, "I think we should kiss again, just to convince everyone we've made up."

"But, Jake—" B.J. started to protest, but he did as he said he would, briefly tasting her lips. Then he lifted his head and smiled into her eyes.

"See? If you could smile instead of looking so stricken, I think we'd be able to convince everyone that you slugged me in a moment of passion." A laughing twinkle in his brown eyes invited her to smile.

She managed a small one, but she also couldn't

help asking the question she'd tried to ask when he kissed her. "Jake, why do we want them to think we've made up?"

"That way, they won't talk about you beating me up."

"Wouldn't it be better for them to think we fought? Then they won't expect anything else from the two of us."

"But then my family will go back to matchmaking," he said as he wrapped his arm around her shoulders and directed her back to the table.

"Jake, I didn't agree to—to help you avoid the matchmaking."

"You sure did. When you agreed that we were together, you signed on, B.J. Unless you want to come right out and tell them we were lying."

She stared at the eager faces of Jake's family, her friends and her aunt, and swallowed. No, she didn't want to tell them she'd lied. But she couldn't keep up the charade if it meant spending time with Jake.

"At least let them believe it for tonight," he whispered. "We don't want to spoil their evening."

She tried to think clearly, but her sensory nerves were on overload and it was hard to clarify anything. They reached the table, and much to her relief, Jake suggested the evening come to an end.

Everyone seemed in agreement. As they stood, B.J. caught sight of Mildred and she remembered the other problem she needed to solve. Mildred and Red.

"Jake," she hurriedly whispered to her escort as

they started toward the door, "can we take the pickup with Red and Mildred?"

She reconsidered the wisdom of her request when Jake stopped to stare at her.

"Good idea," he murmured, a look in his eyes that gave her pause. "That will really convince everyone."

If it hadn't been for Mildred, she would've protested and changed her mind. But she had to do what she could for her aunt.

It took only a couple of whispered conversations on Jake's part before the four of them got into the pickup and headed toward the ranch.

B.J. waited at least five minutes before she ended the tense silence that had prevailed. "Red, Toby and I are the only family Mildred has, and Toby is a little young to assume his responsibilities as the man of the family. So I hope you'll forgive me for asking this question." She paused and studied the man's wary expression. Then, with a big smile, she asked, "What are your intentions toward Mildred?"

"Barbara Jo!" Mildred exclaimed.

Red looked at Mildred and then back at B.J. "I asked Mildred to marry me, B.J. But she turned me down."

"Did she?" B.J. slanted a quick look at Mildred's burning cheeks. "I'm sorry. I would've liked to welcome you to our family, Red. It's too bad she doesn't care enough about you."

Mildred gasped and turned to look out the window.

Red stuck out his chin. "That's not the reason she turned me down."

B.J. was distracted by the truck slowing to a stop on the side of the road.

"We're almost home," Jake said softly. "I thought you might need a little more time."

With a nod, she turned her attention back to the couple behind her. "It's not, Red? Why did she turn you down?"

"That's between me and Red," Mildred protested.

"Normally I would agree, Mildred," B.J. said quietly, "but I suspect Toby and I play a role here. Am I right, Red?"

"You're right," he said succinctly.

B.J. reached over the seat to touch Mildred's hands, clenched tightly in her lap. "Mildred, I can't ever repay you for the support and love you've given me and Toby. Especially right after Darrell died. But we would never want you to sacrifice your happiness for ours."

Mildred lowered her head but said nothing.

"Besides, it's not like you'd go very far," B.J. teased softly. "You could still keep an eye on Toby for me."

"That's what I told her," Red said, hope lightening the expression on his face.

"And what happens when someone calls you in the middle of the night?" Mildred asked forcefully, staring at B.J.

"We'd work something out, Mildred. Surely that's

not enough of a reason to deny Red's happiness. And think how much Toby would enjoy having another man in the family," B.J. added, grinning at Red.

When she looked at Mildred, B.J. felt her heart lurch. Tears were streaming down the older woman's cheeks. Had she gone too far? Would Mildred forgive her?

"Mildred, don't cry. I didn't mean to upset you." She cast a frantic look at Jake, who sat silently beside her. "I think we should go on now."

Without any argument, Jake started up the truck. B.J. turned toward the front, leaving Mildred to Red's whispered reassurances. She only hoped he was able to make Mildred's tears stop.

When they stopped by the ranch house, B.J. spoke again. "Mildred, I'll take Toby home. You and Red may need a little time to talk."

"That boy's getting too big for you to carry. You'll need help," Mildred insisted.

"She's got me." Jake offered. "I can handle Toby, Mildred,"

B.J. opened her mouth to protest, but she paused as she noticed Mildred's acceptance of Jake's words. She could carry Toby. He was only a little boy. But if Jake's offer satisfied Mildred, B.J. wouldn't say anything.

Toby had fallen asleep, of course, and B.J. reluctantly allowed Jake to carry him the short distance to her house. The sight of her little boy wrapped in Jake's strong arms unexpectedly moved her. Perhaps it was because of all the stress of the evening, the assault on her senses.

Whatever the reason, her eyes filled with unshed tears as she watched Jake hold Toby against his broad chest. Her child would never know a father's touch, a father's guidance, as he grew to manhood.

She squared her shoulders. It didn't matter. He would be loved.

"His bedroom is the last one," she whispered as she held open the door for Jake. Toby's bed was ready. She'd turned down the covers before they'd left.

After Jake laid him on the bed, she murmured her thanks, hoping Jake would leave, and tucked the covers around Toby, gently touching his flushed cheek as he lay sleeping. When she straightened and turned around, she discovered Jake leaning against the door frame, watching her.

He stood back to allow her to precede him, then followed her down the hall to the front door.

"Toby's a lucky boy," he said softly as she stopped.

"What do you mean?"

"His mom loves him very much."

"And yours didn't love you?"

His brows arched, as if he were surprised by her response. "Of course she did, but she died."

"How old were you when she died?"

"Eight."

"Toby's father died when he was one. So he's only

had one parent—and who knows what the future holds?''

"That's kind of morbid."

"No, realistic."

"I was trying to pay you a compliment, B.J.," he said with exasperation.

She shrugged her shoulders and looked away. The tenderness in his voice was too much to bear after the events of the night. "Sorry. It's been a difficult evening."

"I appreciate what you did for Red."

"I didn't do anything for Red. I was trying to help Mildred. She deserves to be happy."

"Doesn't everyone?"

Sighing, B.J. gestured to the door. "It's late, Jake. Too late for a philosophical discussion."

"Okay. I can take a hint." He reached out toward her, but she jerked back. "I was only going to touch your cheek, B.J., not retaliate." His lips curved in a teasing grin.

"I've already apologized," she returned abruptly.

"But not explained." Something in her expression must've warned him to save his breath. He held up his hands in surrender and backed out the door. "Okay. I won't mention it again. Good night… partner."

She ground her teeth as she watched his long stride cover the distance between their homes. No, she hadn't explained—and she wouldn't. But she intended to make sure she never got that close to Jake Randall again.

JAKE WAS FEELING pretty pleased with himself as he walked back to his house. He'd foiled the plans of the females of the house. Ceci was as wrong for him as all the other women they'd pushed forward. But thanks to B.J.'s and his fast thinking, he hadn't had to spend the evening avoiding Ceci.

As an extra bonus, he'd shared some interesting moments with B.J. She was sexy as hell—which he'd known the first moment he'd met her. But he'd never been this close to her before. Or tasted those soft lips.

With a rueful laugh, he rubbed his chin. He'd never paid such a price for a kiss before, either. The memory of the emotions that filled him when he'd held her in his arms chased away his amusement.

It was just as well she'd hit him. It was a good warning to keep in mind. He should keep his emotional distance from B.J. But he might forget that fact if he spent much more time kissing B. J. Anderson.

As he stepped up on the back porch, the door opened and Red and Mildred emerged. The only light on the back porch spilled out from the house, but it was enough for Jake to see the bemused expressions of happiness on the couple's faces.

"I'm gonna walk Mildred home," Red said, his gaze meeting Jake's only briefly. The man could hardly keep his eyes off Mildred, whose cheeks were bright red.

"Good. See you in the morning."

The couple passed him, their arms wrapped around each other, and faded into the night. Jake stood there, his hands on his hips, his eyes staring at nothing in the darkness. Looked like Red, too, would be joining the married state. Pretty soon he'd be the last bachelor on the Randall spread. Quite a change from last year at this time, when they'd been all men, all bachelors.

Jake dismissed the feeling of loneliness that assailed him. He was happy. He didn't need the complication of a woman to make his life worthwhile. In fact, in his experience, contrary to his brothers', adding a woman to his life would only bring misery.

Some men weren't meant to be married.

He was one of them.

"MOMMY, YOU DIDN'T KISS me good-night last night," Toby protested from the door, rubbing sleep from one eye.

B.J. smiled at her little boy, in his pajamas, still young enough to enjoy a cuddle from his mommy. Her heart swelled with love as she opened her arms to him. When he raced across the kitchen, she lifted him up and pressed her lips to his cheek.

"Oh, yes, I did. But you were sound asleep." And she'd been glad. After that kiss she'd shared with Jake the night before on the dance floor, she hadn't wanted to face either Toby or Mildred.

"Where's Aunt Mildred?"

B.J. took a deep breath. It was unusual for her aunt

not to be in the kitchen first thing in the morning. Was she angry about last night? "I'm not sure."

Toby didn't show much concern for Mildred's absence. His mind still seemed to be occupied with the previous night. "How did I get in my bed last night? I went to sleep on Mr. Jake's couch."

According to Toby, everything on the Randall ranch belonged to Mr. Jake. B.J. had tried to explain that all four brothers shared the ranch, but Toby knew who was boss.

"Mr. Jake carried you to your bed."

"He did?" Toby asked with awe in his voice. "Just like he was my daddy?"

"No!" B.J. answered sharply, and then regretted her response. Hugging her little boy to her, she kissed him again and said, "Like a friend, Toby. Mr. Jake is a friend."

"I guess he is," a familiar voice said.

B.J. whirled around to find Mildred standing where Toby had been when he first claimed her attention. Thankfully Mildred had a smile on her face.

"I was afraid you were angry with me."

"I should be," Mildred said, but she was still smiling.

Pudgy little hands covered each of B.J.'s cheeks as Toby turned her face to him. "Why would Aunt Mildred be mad at you, Mommy? Did you do something bad?"

B.J. laughed, relief filling her. "Nope." She kissed

his nose and then set him down. "But if I don't turn the bacon, I'll burn it, and you wouldn't like that."

Mildred joined her, apologizing for oversleeping, and together they finished breakfast and sent Toby off to get dressed.

Mildred said nothing about the previous evening, and B.J. hesitated to ask. She'd interfered enough in her aunt's life.

But the look on Mildred's face told of her happiness. B.J. hoped that meant Mildred and Red had worked out their differences. Before she worked up her nerve to ask, Toby burst back into the kitchen in jeans and shirt, his sneaker laces flopping.

"Whoa, young man, you're going to trip if you don't tie your shoes," she warned, and knelt down to provide some motherly assistance.

"Have you told Toby yet?" Mildred suddenly asked.

"Told me what?" Toby asked.

"I thought your mommy might have told you that you're going to have a grandpa." Mildred's cheeks were bright red, but a big smile was on her lips.

"A grandpa?" Toby asked, his eyes round with surprise.

"Would you like that?"

"I guess so," There was doubt in his voice. "How would I get a grandpa?"

"Well, I'm not really your grandma, but that's how I think of myself. So when I marry Red, I guess he'll be your grandpa."

Toby's eyes got even bigger. "You're gonna marry Mr. Red?"

Mildred nodded and let her gaze meet B.J.'s for the first time since she'd announced her intentions.

Still seeing the hesitation in Mildred's eyes, B.J. gave her her biggest smile. "I'm so happy for you, Mildred."

"You're sure we can work things out?"

"Of course we can."

"If you marry Mr. Red, Mr. Jake will be part of our family, too, won't he, Mommy? Will he be my brother?"

B.J. leaned over to smooth Toby's dark hair from his face. "No, sweetie, Mr. Jake won't be your brother."

"But we have the same birthday, and he's my bestest friend. Mr. Jake said he's going to teach me to be a cowboy. The other day he showed me how to rope," Toby said, his face beaming, "'cept I didn't learn too good. But Mr. Jake said—"

"I think maybe we've heard too much about what Mr. Jake said," B.J. said. "But I didn't know your birthdays were the same. Are you sure?"

Toby nodded vigorously.

"Well...that doesn't mean anything. Mr. Jake isn't kin to Red," B.J. hastily explained.

"Don't worry, child," Mildred said, still smiling. "Mr. Jake may be part of your family before you know it."

"Yippee!" Toby shouted.

"Mildred!" B.J. protested.

"Now don't go all coy on me, young lady. I wouldn't have accepted Red's proposal if I hadn't seen the way the winds were blowing last night."

Chapter Five

Last night all Jake's problems had seemed solved. But this morning he wasn't so sure.

B.J. had cooperated, but she'd also indicated her cooperation was a one-shot deal. Jake had thought last night that he could go along with her decision. After all, he wasn't looking for anything permanent.

Now he realized he was going to look like an idiot.

Ever since sunup, his men had been teasing him about B.J. He'd tried to make light of his behavior last night, telling them he still intended to play the field.

They'd laughed at him.

He'd told them he'd never marry.

They'd agreed, then winked at each other.

He had in mind to tell them that B.J. was nothing special.

They wouldn't have believed him. And he didn't blame them. That's why he couldn't say those words. Because he knew B.J. was special. She was a beauty. She was intelligent. She was a great mom.

And the best kisser he'd ever run across.

"Still daydreaming about B.J., boss?" one cowboy called out, and then maneuvered his horse to the other side of the herd they were moving, to make sure he kept some distance between himself and Jake.

"Get to work, you mangy cuss," Jake called back, but he couldn't be angry with the man. He'd brought the teasing on himself by the show he'd put on last night.

Pete pulled up beside him. "The boys are having a lot of fun at your expense, brother. You okay with that?"

"I've teased a few of them in my time. Turnabout is fair play."

"You're better at this game than I am. I guess I was pretty hard to live with before Janie married me."

Jake chuckled. "I believe you could call that an understatement, Pete. You were meaner than a mama bear protecting her cub."

"Aw, I wasn't that bad."

Before Jake could assure his brother that he had been impossible to live with, they were distracted by a shout from one of the cowboys, pointing into the distance.

What had drawn his attention was a truck crossing the pasture, heading in their direction.

"Something wrong at the ranch?" Pete wondered aloud, watching the truck.

Jake frowned as he stared at the approaching vehicle. He was pretty sure he'd identified the driver. He couldn't figure why B.J. felt they should settle their differences in front of his entire staff, but he was afraid that was what she had in mind.

He cleared his throat. "That's B.J. She probably needs to talk to me. You wait here with the boys."

"But it might be something about my herd for the rodeo," Pete said.

"Then I'll call you. Wait here," Jake barked. If he didn't start toward B.J. now, she'd have her truck right next to the herd before she stopped, and they'd have an audience interested in whatever she had to say.

He eased his horse into a lope toward the approaching truck, but he could still hear Pete as he hollered, "I guess you're not as calm as I thought."

He was calm, he assured himself. He just didn't want B.J. telling everyone he'd drafted her into playing a role last night. That was all.

She pulled the truck to a stop and waited for him to reach her. She must not be any more interested in an audience than he was. He swung from the saddle and strode the couple of feet to the door of her truck as she opened it.

"Good mornin', B.J.," he drawled, but his heart sped up as she looked at him, her hazel eyes wide, an anxious look in them. "Everything okay?"

One thing he'd always given B.J. credit for: she was a straight shooter whether you liked it or not. Now his heart double-clutched when she looked away from him.

"Um, not exactly."

"What do you mean? Do they need us at the house?"

"No! Everything's fine." She flashed him a quick look and then stared at the cattle behind him.

"Something wrong with the herd?"

"No."

"Then what in blazes are you doing here, woman?" he asked in exasperation. She was driving him crazy with her evasions...and her soft lips. The urge to kiss her, in broad daylight, startled him.

"I need to talk to you."

"You don't seem to be doing much of that."

Finally she turned to look at him, but anger drove her if her expression was anything to go by. "Give me a break. This is awkward."

"Couldn't it wait until this evening?" he asked testily, figuring he knew what was coming. But he darn sure couldn't see any urgency.

"No! Tonight might be too late."

He cocked one eyebrow at her and took a step closer, moving almost inside the door where she was standing. Just close enough to catch her scent.

"Too late for what?"

"Jake, I have to ask a favor," she said, her voice low, that throaty purr that drove him crazy. She reached out and caught the front of his jacket.

His hand closed over hers, feeling the soft warmth of her skin, wishing she'd slide her hand inside his shirt. Clearing his suddenly hoarse throat, he muttered, "Yeah?"

She drew a deep breath, and he watched the rise and fall of her bosom, feeling like a seventeen-year-old boy, afraid to breathe in case he completely lost control.

"Could we—could we pretend a little longer?"

His mind was so clogged with sensations it took him a minute or two to understand what she'd said. "You want to continue pretending to date?" He shot a quick look over his shoulder to make sure no one could overhear their conversation.

Every man in the saddle was staring at them.

He turned back to B.J., realizing she hadn't answered his question. "Well?"

"Not...exactly."

He released her hand to capture her shoulders. "What are you asking?"

"I need us to pretend to—to be an item."

"An item?" He wanted to be sure he understood what she was asking.

"Stop being obtuse, Jake!" she shouted, and struck his chest.

"Whoa! For someone asking a favor, you're being a little aggressive, aren't you, sweetheart?" He was beginning to enjoy their conversation. He had a feeling he was about to get the upper hand.

"The favor isn't for me, you jerk. It's for Red and Mildred."

Her lips were pressed together, flattening out their

fullness, but he still wanted to feel them beneath his, to taste her sweetness. He was filled with a hunger that had nothing to do with food.

"Well ? Will you agree?" she prodded.

"Why do Red and Mildred care if we... date?"

"Because Mildred won't agree to marry Red unless she thinks—" B.J. broke off and sighed. "I feel utterly outdated by saying this, but Mildred wants to be *sure* I have a man to take care of me before she'll marry Red."

Mentioning marriage in the same sentence with him made Jake nervous. He stepped back. "What do you mean, *sure?* Are you asking me to marry you?"

He hadn't meant to sound as if that prospect ranked lower than being bucked off a bronco onto sharp rocks. But he must've. Her cheeks whitened, and she abruptly slid back into the truck. He grabbed the door before she could slam it shut.

"Wait! I'm sorry, B.J. I didn't mean to—"

"Turn loose!" She tugged on the door, and he instantly remembered how hard she had hit him last night.

He managed to slip his body between her and the door. "No fair running off without finishing our discussion."

When she realized she couldn't budge him, she stared straight ahead, her hands gripping the steering wheel.

"I just wanted to be clear on what you were asking," he said, watching her closely.

With her jaw unclenched just enough to form words, she muttered, "I wanted you to pretend we were serious about—about each other until Red and Mildred get married. Once they're legally tied, we can have a fight—which shouldn't be difficult to arrange—and break it off."

He should have felt relief. He did, he assured himself. She wasn't setting a trap for him. She didn't want marriage any more than he did. It was all pretense.

"Okay."

His brief answer didn't seem to have an effect on her. She continued to stare straight ahead over the steering wheel.

"Well?" he said, hoping for some reaction. "Is that all you wanted?"

"Yes, that's all I wanted. Thank you."

She didn't sound grateful. In fact, she sounded as though she'd prefer to rub his face in the mud of a pigpen. Hell, he was taking a risk just for her. She ought to at least appreciate it!

He remembered that he'd asked her to take the same risk last night without giving her much of an option. But that wasn't the point.

"So you can move now," she ordered, anger still lacing her words.

"Not quite yet." He might as well get some pleasure out of their agreement, especially since he wasn't getting any appreciation. Without any warning, he reached inside the truck, grabbed her by her jacket collar and pulled her from the truck into his arms.

Then his lips did what they'd been wanting to do ever since she arrived. They covered hers, molding her flesh to his, tasting her sweetness. In spite of her anger, her mouth opened to his, welcomed his tongue as he entered, joined in their mating. Her arms encircled his head, her fingers weaving through his hair, knocking his cowboy hat to the ground.

She was wearing those sexy jeans again, and his hands cupped her bottom, pulling her tightly to him, feeling her breasts against his chest. He wanted her naked, wanted to forget everything but her.

But the cheering in the distance brought both of them back to reality. They broke apart simultaneously. Her face was red, and she hid it on his chest.

"I forgot about our audience," he muttered.

"We—we don't need to get so realistic in our pretense in the future," she returned, raising her gaze to his. "Kissing isn't a good idea."

"You weren't objecting a minute ago."

"Well, I'm objecting now." This time when she got into the cab of the truck, he stepped back and she slammed the door.

Then she rolled down the window. "Promise you won't tell anyone what we're doing. Please."

"No one?"

"No one."

He shrugged his shoulders. "Okay, I promise."

She stared at him intently, and his shoulders stiffened. Was she questioning his word? But all she did was nod and throw the truck into reverse.

He watched her drive away, reliving the kiss as he did so. The cool October wind interrupted his pleasure and reminded him that his hat was missing. When he found it on the ground, it had been pancaked by B.J.'s tire.

Shaping it as best he could, he jammed it on his head and turned around to face an appreciative audience.

Somehow he didn't think he and B.J. were going to have to work very hard to spread the word about their...agreement.

B.J. DROVE RAPIDLY across the pasture, bouncing on the seat, too disturbed to slow down. She'd known the conversation would be difficult. Damn that sexy man's hide.

She should be used to the Randalls' handsomeness. Those lean cowboy hips, broad shoulders, all that muscle, topped by warm brown eyes, a lazy grin. One man fitting that description would be spectacular. Four men, each with a big heart and a bright mind, were almost more than a woman could comprehend.

And why one of those men, only one, should have the effect on her that Jake had was inexplicable. She'd known right away that her nervous system went on overload whenever she was around him. Fortunately he'd avoided her.

Until last night.

And look what she'd gotten herself into now. More time spent with Jake. But it was for Mildred's happiness. Once she married Red, then B.J. and Jake would return to their distant relationship. Which would be much easier on her nerves.

THE THREE RANDALL LADIES gathered in the living room, seated close together so as not to be overheard.

"What do you think?" Janie asked, watching her cohorts.

"He certainly took the bait," Megan said, "but will it last?"

"Maybe…if we keep the pressure on. Do we know any more disasters?" Anna asked.

"Just a few," Janie assured her as she rolled her eyes. "And they'd all leap at the chance to spend time with Jake."

"Well, you can't blame them," Megan said with a self-satisfied chuckle. "These Randall men are really something."

"And that's why we've got to marry off Jake. He's too attractive. We'll have a constant stream of women in here trying to attract him. Or any other man they can find."

"You can't fool us, Janie," Anna said softly. "You want Jake to be happy as much as the rest of us."

"Yeah," Janie agreed with a sigh.

B.J. DROVE HOME, contented. She'd just spent the afternoon at the Winstons' helping Grey Winston deliver the first foal bred from his prize stallion. The birth had been difficult, but mother and baby were doing well now. Grey had insisted on opening a bottle of champagne to celebrate.

After a sip, B.J. had excused herself. It was almost six. She tried to be home by five each day, but her job wasn't one for a clock watcher.

Which gave her a good excuse to avoid Jake.

Last night, after her morning talk with him in the pasture, she'd gotten home after eight. Mildred had asked her if she wasn't going to call Jake, but she'd told her she'd talked to him earlier.

If Mildred assumed they'd spent time on the phone exchanging words of love, it wasn't B.J.'s fault. She hadn't said anything like that.

As she pulled up to her house, she checked the rearview mirror, making sure Jake wasn't coming out of his house or the barns. If her luck held, maybe she wouldn't see him until Red and Mildred's wedding.

The only problem was she hadn't gotten a definite date out of Mildred. She'd tried last night, but Mildred had concentrated on feeding her and avoiding an answer.

She opened the door of her truck and got out. Tonight. Tonight she'd press Mildred to set a date for the wedding.

"Anyone home?" she called as she opened the door, expecting Toby's usual greeting.

Toby exploded down the hall. "Mommy! Guess

what! We're eating dinner with Mr. Red and everyone."

"We are?"

"You're not," Mildred said, appearing next with a beaming smile on her face.

"I don't understand."

"Red and I know you and Jake don't get too much time together, so we're going to take care of Toby tonight. We're going to watch a movie after dinner. Then Red and I will come back here and put Toby to bed so you and Jake can stay out as late as you want."

B.J. swallowed, frantically trying to find a way to change the plans. "Jake may have already made plans."

"Red checked with him this morning. Didn't he mention our idea when you talked to him?"

"Uh, no. I guess he forgot." Did Mildred think she and Jake were in constant communication?

"Why can't I go with you and Jake, Mommy?" Toby asked, his arms still around her neck.

Inspiration struck her as she stared into Toby's eager eyes. "I think that's a great idea, Toby. After all, Mildred, you and Red are the couple getting married. You need the time alone."

"Nonsense. Red and I are too old for gallivantin' around. We'll leave that up to you young ones."

"But I don't get to spend much time with Toby. I don't want—"

"We've already got everything arranged. And

you'd better head for the shower. Jake will be here in half an hour.''

"Half an hour?" B.J. asked in shock.

"You'll want to look your best for him. After all, there's lots of women chasing after Jake Randall.'' Mildred stepped forward and pulled Toby out of her arms. "Go figure out which storybook you want to take to show Mr. Red how well you can read, young man. I don't want to be late for dinner, either.''

Toby immediately set off at a run for his bedroom, leaving B.J. standing by the front door still looking for a way out. "But, Mildred—"

"Don't you want to spend time with Jake? I thought you two—"

"Of course I do!" B.J. exclaimed. "You took me by surprise. And—and I worry about Toby.''

"Nonsense, child. He'll be fine with me and Red. You go make yourself pretty for that hunk you've snared.'' Mildred pushed her toward her bedroom, her serenity restored.

But B.J. could barely walk. Her insides were churning, and she was grateful she didn't have to continue her conversation with her aunt. She could scarcely think, much less talk.

And in half an hour, not only did she have to make herself presentable, but she also had to regain her composure. She didn't want Jake to realize how much he affected her.

"YOU'RE NOT GOING to wear that," Red said the moment Jake walked into the kitchen.

Jake came to an abrupt halt and looked down at his jeans and plaid shirt. They looked clean to him. "Why not?"

"'Cause I think B.J. would expect you to dress up a bit. After all, you two haven't gotten away from the family much. Give you a chance to, you know, cuddle." Red dug his elbow into Jake's side.

Jake grabbed Red's arm. "What are you talking about? Is B.J. coming— I mean, are Mildred and B.J. and Toby coming here for dinner?"

"Weren 't you listening this morning, boy? I told you Mildred and I were taking care of Toby so you could take B.J. out."

"No, you didn't! I would've remembered—besides, it's too late. I didn't know, so I didn't ask her. B.J. would slug me again if I asked her out to dinner at this late date. Even *I* know that much about women."

"Not to worry," Red assured him, and calmly returned to the stove. "Mildred took care of it for you. Better go change."

"Change? Change into what? Since you arranged this date, just where am I taking her?"

"There's this new restaurant in Wyndom. It has candles and tablecloths and everything."

"Wyndom? That's fifty miles away."

"That's right. That gives you a nice, long ride

home with the little lady.'' Red winked. ''Now get back up those stairs and put on some fancy duds.''

Jake did as he was told...this time. But he was going to have to get a handle on this pretense. No one was going to lead him around by the nose.

Chapter Six

Jake knocked on the door and then stepped back, drawing a deep breath. Under Red's orders, he'd changed into a tweed sports jacket and white shirt. But he'd kept on his jeans.

After all, this night was B.J.'s idea. So she owed him. And if he wanted to wear jeans, instead of a suit, it was okay.

The door swung open, and Mildred beamed at him. "Come in, you handsome man. Don't you look fine!"

"Evenin', Mildred. Is B.J. ready?"

"I'll go see."

As she turned away, Toby came tearing down the hall, followed by his dog. "Hi, Mr. Jake!"

Jake squatted to the little boy's eye level. "Hi there, Toby. How are you?"

"Great! We're going to eat with Mr. Red. I asked Mommy if I could eat with you, but she said no."

He wouldn't have minded if the little guy came with them. He may have avoided B.J. the past nine months, but he and Toby had become fast friends.

"Next time we'll include you, buddy, okay? I heard they're building a McDonald's in Rawhide."

"Wow! I love McDonald's! Do they have a playground?" Toby asked, his eyes wide with excitement.

"I don't know. We'll check it out."

"Okay! Wait till I tell Mommy."

"Does your mommy like McDonald's?" He didn't know much about B.J.—except that she made his temperature rise.

Before Toby could inform him of B.J.'s tastes, Jake caught movement at the other end of the hall out of the corner of his eye. He looked up and almost fell flat on his back. He'd seen B.J. in snug jeans and a flared denim skirt and blouse, but he'd never seen her dressed in a silk sheath.

He cleared his throat, wondering if she'd intentionally forgotten to fasten the last two buttons on the dress. "Hi, B.J. You look nice."

"Thank you." She came down the hall and knelt down next to Toby and Jake. "Give me a goodbye hug, sweetie. And be good for Aunt Mildred."

Toby slung his arm around his mother's neck and hugged her, leaving Jake an unobstructed view of the top of B.J.'s dress, too. He swallowed, his mouth suddenly dry, as he eyed the shadowy V formed by the valley between her breasts.

B.J. stood and called down the hall, "We're leaving, Mildred."

Jake stood and stepped toward the door.

"Bye, Mr. Jake," Toby said.

The touch of sadness in the little boy's voice had Jake flashing a look of alarm at B.J. "We could change our plans, go somewhere—"

"I already tried. Besides, I can't let Toby con me. He wouldn't have any respect for me. Right, Toby?"

"Aw, Mommy," the little boy protested, but he grinned.

Mildred joined them. "You two get along, now. You don't want to miss your reservation."

Jake stepped aside for B.J. to precede him out the door. Then he followed to open her truck door, receiving a raised eyebrow but no comment from her. Once he got behind the wheel, however, she had a question.

"Reservations? I didn't know there was a restaurant around here that took reservations."

"There's a new restaurant in Wyndom."

"Wyndom? That's fifty miles away."

"I know." He hadn't meant to sound irritated, but he'd already put in a long day. To drive almost an hour just to eat made him weary.

She stared at him, her face expressionless, before saying, "This evening wasn't your idea, was it?"

"Did you think it was? You're the one who asked that we continue the charade. I figured you planned the evening." A quick glance at her had him adding, "Not that I object to spending an evening with a beautiful woman, but..."

B.J. bit down on her bottom lip. "I think I've been had."

"What do you mean?"

"I don't think Mildred believed our story."

Jake shrugged. "It was kind of sudden."

"It was your idea. I guess it wasn't such a good one."

"You didn't think it was at the time. I didn't expect you to want to continue with it." If she was going to criticize him, he wanted to remind her that they were together tonight because of her, not him.

It was dark in the truck, but he could feel her embarrassment. "I didn't know what else to do," she explained stiffly.

He felt like a heel. "Hey, it's no big deal. Relax and enjoy the evening. I owe you one for Friday night, anyway. It would've been a miserable evening with Ceci in pursuit."

B.J. said nothing.

It was going to be a long drive.

BY THE TIME THEY REACHED the restaurant, B.J.'s stomach was tied in knots. A combination of worry about Mildred and worry about resisting Jake's charm made conversation almost impossible with the incredibly handsome man next to her.

"We're here. Let's see if this dinner is worth the drive," Jake drawled, smiling at her, inviting her to share his amusement.

"Yes," she agreed, clearing her throat. She didn't wait for him to come around and open her door. Sliding down from the pickup, she straightened her skirt and turned toward the restaurant door.

"I've never seen you dressed so, uh, nice," Jake said, placing his hand in the small of her back to guide her.

She pulled away.

"B.J., you're going to have to stop acting like I'm poison. Otherwise, people will never believe we're dating."

"I'm not sure that's what we should be doing," she whispered.

He clutched her waist and pulled her to a halt. "Now, wait a minute. Is this the same woman who drove all the way out to the pasture to ask me to cooperate? Isn't that why we're here tonight?"

"I don't know, Jake," B.J. wailed softly. "I'm confused. I think Mildred doesn't believe our story. But should we try to convince her? Or should we give up? I don't know what to do."

Jake tipped up her chin. "We should go inside and enjoy a nice dinner. That's what we should do. We'll decide how to proceed after we eat." He brushed her lips with his. "I'm no good making decisions on an empty stomach."

As if he were sure of her agreement, Jake took her arm and led her toward the door.

Maybe he was right. All this stewing would do her no good. And why waste a good evening? After all, ever since arriving at the ranch, she'd dreamed of a date with Jake Randall.

Not that this was really a date. But she could enjoy it, even so if she'd relax. With a deep breath, she stepped into the restaurant. This far from the ranch, they'd be truly alone, and she planned to enjoy the evening.

Jake echoed her thoughts as he whispered, "We probably won't see anyone we know, anyway."

To their surprise, the lobby of the restaurant was filled with prospective diners. Jake stepped forward and gave his name to the maître d'.

"Of course, Mr. Randall, your table will be ready in just a moment."

Before Jake could turn away, another man approached the maître d'. "Look, we've been waiting for forty-five minutes. Are you sure you don't have anything?"

"Not yet, sir."

"Ben?" Jake recognized his neighbor and longtime friend.

"Oh, Jake, I didn't see you." It was Ben Turnbull, a rancher from near the Randall spread.

"You waiting for a table?"

"Yeah. I hope you don't have much of an appetite, 'cause we've been waiting more than three-quarters of an hour."

"Your table is ready, Mr. Randall," the maître d' said, interrupting them.

Ben shrugged and turned back to join his wife.

"I'm glad Red made a reservation for us," Jake

muttered, taking B.J.'s arm as they followed in the wake of their guide.

"That was Ben Turnbull, wasn't it?" B.J. asked. She'd met the man once before, but not his wife.

"Yeah. They've been waiting for a table for forty-five minutes."

They reached a secluded table for four.

Jake's gaze met B.J.'s, a question in it.

She frowned, sure it wouldn't be a good idea to offer to share their table, but like Jake, she couldn't refuse. "Of course."

Jake smiled and turned to the maître d'. "Would you ask Mr. Turnbull if he and his wife would like to join us?"

The man nodded and hurried back to the front of the restaurant. Almost immediately the Turnbulls joined them.

"Jake, are you sure we're not intruding?"

"Not at all. Hello, Lucy. Have you met B. J. Anderson?"

The two women exchanged greetings and sat down. B.J. liked the friendliness of the other woman. Though she'd met most of the men in the county, she hadn't come into contact with many of the women.

"We're celebrating our wedding anniversary," Lucy confessed shyly after their orders had been taken. "We've been married three years."

There was a glow on her face that told B.J. the romance certainly hadn't gone out of her marriage. It gave B.J. an unexpected hunger for that contentment.

Her own marriage had been a good one, the short time it had lasted. But she and Darrell had been friends more than passionate lovers.

Ben reached out and took Lucy's hand. "We're celebratin' something else, too. Can I tell 'em, sweetheart?" She nodded, and Ben added, "We're going to have a baby. We just found out today."

"Congratulations," Jake offered, a big smile on his face. B.J. added hers, also.

"I guess you know a lot about babies now, Jake, don't you? What with all your brothers' doings."

"Well, Ben, I know a lot more than I did last year at this time. We've got the twins, you know, and then Megan's expecting in about six weeks."

"How exciting," Lucy said softly.

"Yes, ma'am, it's exciting, all right. The next generation of Randalls. Our ranch has been passed down from father to son for four generations. I didn't want that to stop."

"That's why Jake set out to matchmake," Ben added, a grin on his face. "Right, Jake?"

B.J. watched Jake, fascinated with the man beside her. She hadn't seen him interact with others much, just his brothers.

Now his cheeks reddened, and he looked hurriedly at B.J. before turning back to Ben. "I don't know that I'd call it matchmaking, Ben. Just a little nudge in the right direction. And Pete managed on his own."

"Yeah, with Janie's help," Ben agreed with a laugh.

"Are you and B.J. celebrating something?" Lucy asked.

B.J., thinking about the Randall brothers, froze, almost choking on the drink of water she'd just taken. "No!" she protested.

"Yeah," Jake contradicted. "We're celebrating getting away from the family." With a grin, he added, "They're a great bunch, but at the rate we're growing, they're a real crowd."

"Ah. You two wanted to be alone, and here we are horning in," Ben concluded.

"No, no, that's not a problem," B.J. hurriedly said. "It was the lure of real tablecloths that got me." She offered a smile and desperately tried to think of a change of subject.

Ben roared with laughter. "Yeah, I bet! I can just see Jake Randall yearning for real tablecloths."

"Now, Ben, stop teasing. These two should be able to enjoy a night out without having to offer an explanation. I'm just glad you decided to share your table. I get tired so quickly these days," she said, smiling at B.J.

Seizing the topic of pregnancy, B.J. talked to Lucy about the difficulties of having a baby, and the two men dealt with ranch topics.

Just as B.J. was beginning to feel comfortable, Lucy leaned closer and asked, "How long have you two been dating?"

"N-not long," B.J. stammered. "We're really just friends."

Lucy smiled. "That may be true, but I haven't seen Jake out with a woman since—why, I guess, since his divorce, five years ago."

"I'm sure he's, uh, dated some since then. Probably in Casper or—or somewhere."

"Jake?" Lucy asked, leaning toward the men and interrupting their conversation. B.J. wanted to shush her, but she couldn't figure how to do it without calling more attention to the topic.

"Yeah, Lucy?"

"I don't recall you dating anyone since your divorce. Until tonight, that is. Am I right?"

B.J. wanted to die of embarrassment as Jake stared at her. She knew he must be wondering what she was doing.

"I think you're right, Lucy. I was kind of snake-bitten after Chloe."

"I don't blame you," Ben said with a shudder. "Beautiful woman, but not our kind."

"Nope. Not our kind," Jake agreed, his gaze still on B.J. She shrugged her shoulders, trying to tell him she hadn't intended to put him on the spot.

"You've made a better choice this time around. B.J. is a great lady," Ben added with a grin.

"She's no slouch in the looks department, either," Jake said. He, too, was grinning, and B.J. wanted to strangle him.

She murmured a thank-you and said a silent prayer of gratitude that their orders arrived to end the conversation. Perhaps if she ate in a hurry, the evening could end before any more damage was done.

After a few minutes, Lucy brought the conversation around to Anna, Jake's sister-in-law. "Do you think Anna will take me on as a patient?"

"I'm sure she will."

"I heard she was cutting back since her marriage to Brett."

Jake answered. "You're close by. I'm sure she'll want to help you out. Unless she's expecting herself."

"Oh? You wanting more babies, Jake?" Ben asked.

"You can't have too many babies. We want the Randalls to continue for generations to come."

"Good thing the first two were boys, then. What if you had all girls? I hope ours is a boy."

B.J. wondered what Jake's response would be. Not that it mattered, but she hated the way some men only wanted sons.

"Same blood, whether it's a boy or a girl, Ben. It's your family. That's what counts." With a sigh, Jake added, "In fact, I think I might like a little girl. They're awful sweet."

"Maybe you should have one yourself," Lucy suggested, with a sly look at B.J.

Though his gaze settled on B.J.'s red cheeks, Jake said, "Nah. I'm not suited to marriage. We've already proved that the hard way."

"Jake, you just made the wrong choice," Ben insisted. "B.J.'s not like Chloe."

"The weather has certainly been nice this fall," B.J. said in strangled tones. Her attempt to steer the conversation in another direction was a total failure.

Ben grinned at her. "Sorry, B.J. I didn't mean to embarrass you, but this guy deserves happiness like the rest of us."

She was at a loss as to how to respond.

"B.J.'s a little shy," Jake said, grinning. "I don't think she's dated much since her husband died."

B.J. almost groaned out loud. Jake had managed to shift the conversation from himself to her, but the topic remained the same.

"When did your husband die?" Lucy asked.

B.J. couldn't refuse to answer, not with the sympathetic smile Lucy offered her. "Four years ago. About six months after our son was born."

"You have a little boy? I didn't know that. So he's four?"

B.J. nodded.

Jake joined in. "Yeah, Toby's a neat kid. And growing like a weed. Did you notice, B.J.? I think he's grown almost a foot since you moved in."

She nodded again.

"I gave Toby one of Molly's pups, and you never see one without the other except for the hours he's at school."

"It's hard being an only child," Lucy said. "I was so lonely until I started school. We don't want our baby to be an only."

B.J. hadn't wanted Toby to be an only child, either,

but sometimes life had other plans than the ones you made. She looked up and realized Jake's gaze was on her. She looked back down at her food.

"It's not too late for B.J. to have more children, either," Ben offered, as if that idea had just occurred to him. "After all, you're not exactly over the hill, B.J."

"Thank you," she murmured. "This food is certainly delicious. Jake, I hope you think it was worth the drive. He was questioning the wisdom of driving this far for a dinner just before we got here." This conversational gambit was more successful than the weather had been earlier. But B.J. was beginning to wonder if their dinner companions would discuss anything but weddings and babies.

Just as they took up the topic of food, they were interrupted by several older couples from Rawhide who were leaving.

"Jake! Good to see you. Well, hi, Ben, Lucy. And B.J., what are you doing— You and Jake are together? Good job, Jake," Henry Pollard roared with a voice loud enough to imitate a bullhorn.

B.J. cringed and tried to appear indifferent to the announcement. Probably no one else knew them here. But she felt the center of attention.

"Just having a meal out, Henry," Jake responded, standing, as did Ben, to shake their hands.

B.J. recognized the other couple and felt her heart sink. Mr. Miller ran the feed store, and his wife was the postmistress for the county. She handed out gossip with the stamps she sold.

"Well, I declare," Mrs. Miller said, smiling at B.J. "I knew the Randall ranch was a hotbed for Cupid, but I never suspected Jake would fall to one of those little arrows."

"We're just having a meal out," B.J. said more forcefully than she should have.

"Oh, of course," Mrs. Pollard agreed, and winked at Mrs. Miller. "Nice choice of companion, though. He's number one on the bachelor list, now that his brothers have been taken."

Before B.J. could protest again, which was probably just as well, Mrs. Pollard turned to Lucy.

"And how are you, Lucy, dear? I heard you were in town today. Everything all right?"

"You were in town and didn't come to see me?" Mrs. Miller asked.

B.J. knew the woman hated to be the last one to know something. She wondered if Lucy would share her news.

"I had to make a quick trip. I'll be back in next week for a real shopping trip and I'll stop by then, Mrs. Miller. I need a new supply of stamps."

"Good. I'll look forward to a little chat. Well, we must go now. Come along, dear," Mrs. Miller said, tugging on her husband's arm.

B.J. had no doubt she was anxious to get outside, where she and Mrs. Pollard could discuss Jake's venture into the dating game. Poor Jake. She remembered his suggestion that they eat and *then* decide whether to continue the charade.

Now it appeared the decision had been made for them.

When they finally left the restaurant, after Jake and Ben amicably argued over who should pay the bill, B.J. breathed a sigh of relief. But she was worried about Jake's reaction to the events of the evening.

He might not have wanted to continue pretending to be involved with her, but rumor would link them together for months to come. Unless he took up with another woman.

That thought bothered B.J., but she didn't want to examine why. Jake wasn't her property.

What would he say about tonight?

They settled into the pickup. Instead of driving off at once, however, Jake sat back and let the engine warm up. B.J. said nothing, waiting for him to speak.

"Interesting evening," he finally murmured.

Warily she nodded, taking one hurried glance at his face before staring out at the cars around them.

He turned toward her, and she held her breath. But the words that came out weren't what she expected.

"Do you want to have another baby?"

Chapter Seven

He watched her reaction to his question. In the dim
light provided by the neon sign outside the restaurant,
he saw her cheeks flush. Her wide stare quickly
shifted to the cars in the parking lot.

"Why—why do you ask?"

He gave an uncomfortable chuckle. "Don't get me
wrong. I'm not volunteering. It just struck me that—
Never mind." He put the truck in gear and began
driving out of the parking lot.

Out of the darkness, B.J.'s soft, sexy voice answered, "Yes, I did want to have more children. I
love Toby, and as Lucy said, it's hard to be an only."

"You were an only child?"

"Yes."

"You and your husband planned on a big family?"

She shifted in her seat, as if she were uncomfortable. Jake stared at her in the darkness, trying to see
her face.

"We really hadn't planned that far ahead," she finally said, her voice calm, emotionless.

He frowned, suddenly filled with a lot of questions about B.J.'s marriage. But he couldn't ask them. Finally he cleared his throat and said, "Toby's a great kid."

"Thank you."

They rode in silence until Jake introduced the subject he figured B.J. wanted to avoid. "So, I guess we're going ahead with the pretense?"

"Do we have any choice? By noon tomorrow, Mrs. Miller will have told everyone in the county that we were out together tonight."

"We could have a big fight, break up."

"We tried that Friday night."

He chuckled. "No, *you* tried it Friday. It wasn't a joint effort."

"True. You were too busy polishing your image as a Romeo," she said stiffly.

"Hey, I had to do something. You slugged me in front of everyone. And then drove all the way out to the pasture to argue with me in front of my crew."

"I didn't come out to argue with you," she protested. "I came out to ask for your cooperation."

"Humph!"

They covered a few more miles in silence.

"I'm sorry, Jake," she finally said, her voice low. He leaned toward her, not sure he'd heard her.

"What?"

"I said I'm sorry. I didn't mean to—to argue with you. I'm not used to negotiating with anyone, much less...a man."

"Did you and your husband always get along?"

"No. But it's been a long time. And—and we don't have a relationship, you and I. There aren't any rules."

Yeah, he knew. He didn't have the right to haul her into his arms and kiss the daylights out of her because he was frustrated. And he was frustrated.

"Guess we'd better work out the parameters fast," he drawled.

"I think it would be best to avoid kissing from now on," she said hurriedly, as if she'd thought of that idea for a while.

"Why? No one will believe we're—how did you put it, an item?—if we don't." And he'd lose out on a lot of pleasure. Kissing B.J. was quickly becoming addictive.

"Yes, they will. You've kissed me enough in front of people that they will assume we're kissing in private."

"Nope." He spoke firmly, determined not to lose this battle. "I'm the kind of guy who touches people. Everyone knows that. If I don't touch you, kiss you, no one will believe our story."

She didn't speak, and he wondered why. He actually began to slow down, considering pulling off the road to check on her when she said, "All right, but keep it to a minimum."

"Why? Don't you want to convince Red and Mildred? Red knows me better than anyone."

"Jake, you're being difficult. You can see that our

kissing all the time could cause problems. You're not a child.''

"Are you telling me that my kissing you gets you stirred up? Heats your blood to a boil?" He was grinning, enjoying her discomfiture. Glad he wasn't the only one turned on.

"And I suppose it doesn't bother you?"

"Lady, one kiss from you and my jeans are too tight. I lay awake at night thinking about you in bed beside me. I'm losing sleep and my appetite just thinking about kissing you."

A car passed by them, and he saw the stunned look on B.J.'s face. She was surprised? He must be a better actor than he'd thought.

"Then why—"

"Why kiss you any more? Because I'm a kissaholic when it comes to you. I can't resist. Besides, we'll never convince Red and Mildred without some kissing." He kept his hands tightly grasped around the wheel. All this talk of kissing made him want to reach out and pull her to him, to pull to the side of the road and follow his talk with action.

"I don't think I can do this."

"Why?" he snapped back, afraid she was getting cold feet.

She didn't answer him.

"You afraid you'll lose control and go too far?"

"Yes! Yes, that's exactly what I'm afraid of."

"So what if you do? You're not a cowering virgin, B.J. Do you intend to go the rest of your life without sex? Sounds mighty sterile to me." His heart was beating faster. He hadn't thought about an affair with her, but now that the possibility had entered his head, he couldn't see any reason not to.

"I don't have affairs," she said icily.

"Have you noticed a parade of women going in and out of *my* bedroom? If you're concerned about a disease, don't be."

She gasped. "You think that's the only reason not to fall in bed with you? That disease is all I have to consider?"

"What else is there? We're attracted to each other. We'd be discreet."

"Everyone in the county already knows we're dating. Is that being discreet?"

"Probably not, but they're going to think we're doing something anyway. We might as well enjoy it." The more he thought about it, the more perfect it sounded. Except...

For the very reason that he hadn't had an affair since his divorce.

Could he handle it? That question stopped him cold. What was he talking about? Of course he could. Couldn't he? He wouldn't get emotionally involved It would just be sex. Plain and simple.

Only sex was never plain and simple.

And as badly as he wanted her now, was it possible he could become addicted to holding her, touching her, kissing her?

Yup. Entirely possible.

He began to sweat.

"Having second thoughts?"

Her soft, sultry voice only underlined his thoughts.

"Maybe. We might get in over our heads."

She responded by laughing, only there wasn't much humor in the sound. "What you're really saying is you're afraid I'll trap you into marriage. That the great Jake Randall might fall into the very trap he set for his brothers."

"Not going to happen, B.J. And you need to understand that up front. Whatever pretending we do, it's not going to lead to marriage," he assured her harshly.

"You sound like you think I *want* to marry you! I can assure you I have no intention of marrying." She crossed her arms under her breasts.

Jake took a deep breath and turned his gaze on the road. Otherwise, he might run them off into a ditch, just thinking about touching that part of her anatomy. Unbuttoning that silk dress, button by button, peeling back the—

"Jake! What's the matter with you?"

"Nothing. I'm not used to having serious discussions while I'm driving." He couldn't come up with a better excuse on short notice.

"But when else can we come to a decision? There's always someone around at the ranch."

"What decision are we coming to?" he asked, distracted every time he looked at her. "Pretending to be together…or being together."

"Temporarily," she added, imitating his slow drawl.

"What?"

"Being together temporarily. In other words, having an affair."

"Is that what we've decided?"

"No! I meant those were our choices. And I refuse to have an affair. I told you."

"So we have no choice. Discussion ended." He figured he was the more frustrated of the two of them, but she didn't sound very happy.

"No, we have another choice. We can choose not to—to pretend. We can stop this nonsense."

"Aren't you forgetting something?" He realized abandoning their scheme would be best. Already he'd discovered she was too potent for pretense. But somehow he couldn't quite give up touching her.

"You mean Mildred and Red?" she asked, her voice falling.

"Yeah. I thought you said they deserve happiness." He slanted a glance her way. "Mildred really made a difference when your husband died, didn't she?"

B.J. didn't say anything for several miles, staring out the window into the darkness. Finally, tucking her chin down, she said softly, "She did. I owe her a lot."

"Then I reckon maybe you owe her our little pretense. It's not going to hurt anyone. The two of us may have to exercise a little extra control, but that's no big deal. I can if you can." He hoped like hell he was right.

Or maybe he hoped he was wrong and *she* couldn't control herself. It wouldn't be his fault if she asked to have sex with him.

That thought brought a big smile to his face.

"What's so funny?" she demanded.

"Nothing," he assured her as a big truck blew past them. He pretended to concentrate on his driving. When she said nothing else, he asked, "So, did you decide?"

"I guess—I guess we should pretend. For a little while longer. As long as it doesn't hurt anything. Don't you think?"

That was the most indecisive he'd ever heard B.J. be. Usually she made quick decisions. He'd admired that in her. But there was something about B.J. tonight, her softness, her sexiness, that was lighting him up. He couldn't really see her in the dark, but her image was imprinted on his brain.

"Okay." He affected a nonchalant tone.

"But you promised to keep the kissing to a minimum," she hurriedly added.

"Right. We don't want anyone to get the wrong idea."

"Right."

But there was a breathless quality to her answer that told him she couldn't help thinking about their kisses.

Silence reigned until they reached home.

Jake parked the truck in its customary spot, rather than parking in front of B.J.'s house. It was only a matter of a few yards. "I'll walk you home," he said as they both got out of the truck.

"That's not necessary." She hurriedly rounded the truck.

"Yes, it is. Red and Mildred are going to be waiting."

"But surely…do you think they'll be watching?"

"Could be. Come here," he ordered, but he actually crossed the distance between them before she could move. He draped his arm across her shoulders and began walking slowly toward her house.

"I'm not sure this is necessary."

"I believe it is. And I think you should wrap your arm around my waist. Red insinuated we should've cuddled in the truck on the drive home. If we'd done that, you wouldn't be standoffish."

"Oh?" she asked, turning to look at him. "All your dates cuddle readily?"

"Yes, ma'am. Satisfaction guaranteed," he assured her, a broad grin on his face. "Want me to demonstrate?"

He lowered his head toward hers, but she pulled away and ran the few short steps to her house.

He caught her hand as she reached the steps, pulling her off balance into his arms. She settled against him as her breath escaped. "Sorry, didn't mean to take your breath away," he assured her, still grinning. In truth, that's just what he wanted to do.

The door opening stopped him from kissing her.

"Have a good time?" Mildred asked from the door, with Red standing beside her.

"Yes," B.J. answered as she pushed against Jake's chest, trying to signal him to release her.

He ignored her and smiled at the other couple. "It's a nice restaurant. You should take Mildred there sometime, Red."

"I'll do that." Red leaned back and chastely kissed Mildred before coming down the steps past them. "Don't mind me. Go ahead and kiss her a time or two." With those instructions, he headed for the Randall house, and Mildred stepped inside and closed the door.

Jake immediately bent to act upon those orders, but B.J. put her hand between their lips just in the nick of time. "They're gone. We don't have to kiss."

Oh, yes, they did. With her pressed against him, kissing was the least of what he wanted to do. "They're probably watching. By now Red's reached the window over the kitchen sink." He glanced toward B.J.'s. "I just saw the lace curtain twitch in your house. Want to bet Mildred's not watching?"

She started to turn her head, to see if she could see the curtain moving, but he stopped her by catching her face in his hands and lowering his lips to hers. Heaven. The long wait since yesterday morning in the pasture was over.

Her soft, warm lips molded to his, and he let his hands wander down the silk that covered her, memorizing the wonderful curves. He deepened the kiss, wanting to touch and feel every inch of her. It was like a craving he'd had for chocolate ice cream as a boy. He'd almost made himself sick eating it, but he'd still wanted more.

And he wanted more of B.J.

HE'D PROMISED!

B.J. kept repeating that protest in her head. But her heart wasn't listening. Or maybe it was her body that urged her closer and closer in Jake's embrace. Her arms stole around his neck, and she opened to his urging.

His kisses were like bolts of lightning running through her, electrifying her body. His hands set her on fire, doubly so when he covered her breast with one of them, massaging and stroking her until she thought she'd explode.

When his lips left hers to trail kisses down her neck, one of his hands began unbuttoning her dress. She covered his hand with hers, knowing she couldn't let him disrobe her outside her house, and lured his lips back to hers.

Only as a distraction, of course.

Only to keep him from venturing other places.

Only to keep her sanity.

"Let's go inside," Jake whispered between kisses.

Inside. Inside with Mildred. And Toby.

"No! No, *I* have to go inside, but you should go home. I—I think we've been more than convincing," she whispered, pressing her hands against his chest, urging him to let her go.

Before she forgot she had to go.

"We need to rethink things," Jake whispered. He wasn't attempting to kiss her lips again, but he hadn't released her either. In fact, he was kissing her neck again.

"R-rethink what?"

"The affair."

"We're not having an affair!" she quickly reminded.

"That's what we need to rethink."

This time she shoved harder and gained a couple of inches as he looked at her. "No. No, we can't rethink that. And we can't k-kiss like this."

"But we have to convince Red and Mildred."

"Did you believe Red loves Mildred?"

"Yes, of course. You know he does."

"Have you ever seen him kiss Mildred like—like you just kissed me?" She sure hadn't.

"No, but I imagine they do when no one's looking. Just because they're older than us doesn't mean—"

"I'm not talking about their age! I'm saying we don't need to kiss like you just kissed me. You could just hug me or something."

"Hug you? I hug Janie and Megan and Anna. I hug Mrs. Miller sometimes, too. I hug Toby. I hug my brothers. How is that going to make someone believe I'm having an affair with you?"

"I don't *want* them to think we're having an affair!'' she said, almost choking on her words. The man was going to give her a heart attack.

"You're asking an awful lot, B.J."

"What do you mean?"

He lifted his hand from her shoulder and stroked his thumb across her cheek. "You want people to believe that we, uh, care about each other...but we're not doing anything about it? We're not inexperienced teenagers."

"We're not animals in heat, either!" she returned hotly.

He looked as though he might argue that point, and she held her breath. She wasn't sure she could come up with logic after the way she'd reacted to his kiss.

A lopsided grin covered his face, making her want to kiss him again. "Well, now, the problem is my reputation is going to suffer."

"What are you talking about?"

"I haven't had a girlfriend in a while. People are going to think I've forgotten what to do with one."

"Jake, you're being ridiculous!"

"Maybe. Maybe I'm trying to figure a way out of our situation without going crazy. Holding you like this and not doing anything about it isn't easy."

She tried to put more space between them, but he resisted. "Wouldn't it be easier if you turned me loose?" she whispered.

"Yeah." His grin widened. "But not near as much fun."

"Jake, you're impossible," she protested, but she couldn't help smiling back at him.

"Yeah, I know. My brothers have told me."

He still held her against him, and she was reluctant to break contact with him, in spite of the shivers that were coursing through her. Finally she pulled away again, and this time he let her go.

"Are we going to be able to do this?" she asked, drawing a deep, shuddering breath, feeling the cool night air now that she was no longer pressed against his heated body.

Again he ran his thumb over her cheek. "Yeah, baby, we can do this. For Red and Mildred, we can do this."

She nodded, unable to say anything.

He leaned over and briefly, oh so briefly, kissed her again. A kiss almost as chaste as the one Red had given Mildred.

When he pulled away, several feet away this time, he gave her another lopsided grin. "I think we just need to practice, that's all."

Then, with a wave, he turned away and strode across the yard to his house.

B.J. stood there, in the deep Wyoming night, watching him walk away. Wondering how she'd survive any more practice as potent as tonight's had been.

Chapter Eight

Jake was late down to breakfast the next morning, an unusual occurrence. But he'd had trouble sleeping after his evening with B.J.—and his night without her.

"Gettin' lazy in your old age, brother?" Chad asked as he entered the kitchen.

"It's not his old age," Pete drawled. "It's starting up with a woman again. You know how that cuts up your peace, Chad."

The three women at the table, Anna, Megan and Janie, protested Pete's words, but Jake ignored all of it. He was busy filling a coffee mug. He needed some caffeine.

"Jake, Halloween's almost here," Janie suddenly said.

He approached the table, his coffee in his hand, and raised one eyebrow at his sister-in-law. "And?"

"I wondered about a Halloween party."

"A party? Haven't we entertained enough this year with all the weddings?" He sat down and began heaping his plate with scrambled eggs and sausage.

"But, Jake," Megan protested, "we could combine Halloween with your birthday."

His head snapped up. "My birthday?" He stared at his three brothers. "Who's been talking?"

"Is it a secret?" Anna asked. "I think it's nice to celebrate together."

Jake couldn't complain after Anna's words. They all knew she'd had no family until she joined theirs. "No, Anna, it's not a secret, but, well, I guess I'm getting to the age that celebrating a birthday isn't that important."

"But it would be fun. Couldn't we have a party?"

Jake groaned. He couldn't say no. "If you want to, I don't mind. But I don't see any reason to include my birthday."

"Well, we were going to celebrate yours and Toby's birthdays together. They're the same day. That's how we knew. Toby told us," Janie explained.   Jake grinned. He'd told Toby a month ago that they shared the same birthday, October 27. He enjoyed the time he spent with the little guy. "He's young enough to be excited about birthdays."

"But he's even more excited about sharing his day with you," Megan explained. "If we celebrate his birthday without celebrating yours, he'll be upset."

Jake sighed and chewed his eggs. Finally he swallowed and looked up to see his family watching him. "Fine. Have a party."

"Thanks, Jake," Anna said with a grin.

His brothers stood up, ready to go to work, and he

hastily took another bite before joining them. At least he wouldn't have to worry about matchmaking since he and B.J. were pretending.

He'd just have to worry about staying in a state of frustration and getting no sleep.

When the door closed behind the four brothers, the three women grinned at each other.

"Perfect. He agreed. Does everyone have a list ready?" Janie asked.

"Yes, but Jake's not going to want to see Mindy again," Megan said.

"We can't worry about what Jake wants," Janie said. "We have to keep the pressure on so he'll hold on to B.J."

"I agree," Anna said. "They're so cute together."

"All right," Megan agreed. "We all invite every bachelorette we know."

"Yeah," Janie agreed, a grin on her face, "it's going to be a real scary Halloween for Jake."

"HAVE YOU AND RED SET a date yet?" B.J. asked her aunt the morning after her dinner with Jake.

"Not yet. I guess we'd better hurry before you and Jake beat us to it. Last night it looked like the two of you were gettin' pretty cozy."

"What's 'cozy' mean?" Toby asked as he scooped his cereal into his mouth.

"Don't talk with your mouth full," B.J. immediately said, casting a warning look at Mildred.

Toby chewed and then repeated his question.

"That means they're being friendly," Mildred explained.

"Then me and Mr. Jake are cozy, too," Toby said with satisfaction. "He's going to take me to McDonald's."

"I'm not sure—" B.J. began. She thought it would be a good idea to cushion her son, in case McDonald's didn't work out.

Toby interrupted her. "Mr. Jake always does what he says, Mommy. Mr. Red told me."

She immediately thought of the good-night kiss last night. He'd promised to keep the kisses to a minimum, but she didn't think that kiss could be considered minimal in any way. She sighed. Maybe next time he would—

"You okay?" Mildred asked, watching her.

"Yes, of course. Well, it's almost time for school. Better go get ready, Toby."

"Okay. Don't forget about making cupcakes for my birthday at school, Aunt Mildred. And make an extra one for Mr. Jake, 'cause it's his birthday, too."

"Land's sake, boy, we've got more than a week before your birthday. I'll get those cupcakes made on time. Don't you worry about it."

Toby grinned and rushed from the room.

B.J. realized she'd have to pull herself together and plan a party for her little boy. And figure out what to buy him for his birthday.

"When are you going to go shopping?" Mildred asked.

B.J. smiled. Trust Mildred to read her mind. "I don't know. And I don't have any idea about what to get him. Got any suggestions?"

"How about a sexy nightgown?"

B.J. stared at her aunt, wondering if she'd lost her mind.

Mildred grinned. "I'm not talking about Toby's birthday present. I'm talking about Jake."

"You think I should get *Jake* a sexy nightgown?"

"I think that's what he'd like…as long as you were wearing it."

"Mildred!"

"Don't you go playing the innocent with me, Barbara Jo," Mildred said, her cheeks almost as red as B.J.'s. "I peeked at the two of you on the porch."

Flashes of the time spent outside with Jake last night did nothing to ease B.J.'s embarrassment. Desperately she sought for a reason to dismiss Mildred's assessment of their relationship. "Jake isn't—"

Footsteps sounded on the porch steps. Mildred leaned back to look out the window. "Jake is here. Guess he couldn't wait to see you."

B.J. jumped up from her chair, her mind frantically looking for reasons for Jake's arrival. "Probably there's a problem with the herd." She tried to ignore Mildred's knowing smile as she left the kitchen.

She swung open the door just as Jake had raised his fist to knock. "Hi. Is something wrong?"

"Nope. How did you know I was here?"

"Mildred saw you. She thinks— Never mind.

What is it?'' She gnawed on her bottom lip, anxiously waiting his response.

He reached out and ran his thumb along her lip. "Don't do that. Or I'm going to swallow you whole."

Jerking back, she pressed her lips together, hoping to convince him that his words didn't affect her at all.

"I needed to talk to you," he finally said.

"Now? Here? But—"

"Why don't you walk over to the barn with me? You can tell Mildred I wanted you to look at one of the mares."

Grateful for his suggestion that implied a return to normalcy, him the rancher, her the veterinarian, she slipped through the door and closed it behind her.

Silently they crossed the yard and entered the horse barn. As soon as the door closed behind them, she whirled around and asked again, "What is it?"

"I just thought I'd tell you that the girls are planning a Halloween-birthday party. I'm sure they think we're together and will expect you to-to look forward to the party."

"Okay." She kept trying to figure out why he thought it necessary to tell her that first thing this morning. It wasn't as if she'd throw up her hands in horror if one of her friends mentioned the party. "Is that all?"

"They may expect you to buy me a birthday present," he added, seemingly a little embarrassed.

B.J. knew her cheeks were bright red, but she couldn't help thinking about Mildred's suggestion.

"I've already discussed that with Mildred." Then she wished she'd kept her mouth closed.

"Oh? Did Mildred have any ideas?"

"Nothing that would work. I don't suppose you could give me any ideas?" That would be a help, since she couldn't think of a single thing to get him. And she hoped her question would distract him from what Mildred had suggested.

"Anything will do. I'll pay you for it as soon as you buy something."

She stared at him. "Why would you do that?"

He shrugged his shoulders. "No reason for you to waste your money on a gift for me."

She was amazed to see his cheeks redden, as if her buying something for him would embarrass him. "Do your brothers give you presents?"

"We never did much for birthdays. We were a houseful of men, you know. Dad usually gave us each a savings bond."

B.J. stared at him, picturing a little boy Toby's age receiving a savings bond as his only birthday present. "Toby wouldn't be satisfied with a piece of paper," she murmured, smiling wryly at Jake.

"I need some ideas about a present for Toby," Jake immediately said, a smile lighting his face.

"He likes toy trucks." She couldn't help smiling back. "How about you? Do you like trucks?"

"Only big ones."

"Mmm," she said, chuckling. "I think a big one is out of my price range."

"That's okay. Mine is in good shape. And I think I'd rather have something else from you." The light in his eyes gave her a hint of his meaning.

"Like what?"

"Let's go back to what Mildred suggested."

"What are you talking about?" she said, but she turned to study the saddle hanging on the wall rather than look at him.

"I'm not sure. But whatever it is sure makes you blush. I figured it must be pretty good."

"Jake, you're teasing me. Don't you have to get to work?" One thing she already knew about the big, handsome cowboy—he loved to tease.

"I guess you're right. My brothers were already curious when I told 'em to go on without me."

"Then I'll be on my way, too. I've got some calls to make."

When she started to move past him, he reached out and caught her shoulders. "Wait a minute. I've been good. I think I deserve a goodbye kiss."

She swallowed, her throat suddenly dry. "There's no one around to impress. I don't see any reason to—"

"I do."

His lips covered hers. Groaning, she gave herself up to the magical touch that always sent her heart soaring. She slid her hands across his chest, beneath his jacket, indulging her needs.

"Mommy, Aunt Mildred said—"

Toby's piping voice intruded upon her bliss. She

ripped herself from Jake's embrace to find her little boy staring up at the two of them.

"Hi, Mr. Jake. Why are you kissing my mommy?"

JAKE ALWAYS ENJOYED spending time with Toby. But he wished the boy had arrived five minutes later. That might've given him enough time to enjoy B.J.'s kiss.

Instead, he noticed the stricken expression on B.J.'s face. Squatting down, he scooped Toby up in his arms, bringing him to his eye level. "Well, Toby, that's something men do when they think a lady is pretty."

Toby gave him a doubtful look. "I think Amber Lloyd is pretty, but I don't kiss her."

"Right, son. That's because you're not grown-up. When you're a man—" he paused and looked at B.J., then turned back to Toby "—you sometimes kiss a lady because she's special."

"Mommy's special," Toby said, nodding.

"My thoughts exactly," Jake agreed.

"Why are you here, Toby? What did Mildred want?" B.J. said abruptly, avoiding Jake's eyes.

"She said I should see if you're taking me to the bus stop this morning. If you're busy, she said she could." Toby didn't even bother to look at his mother. He was examining Jake's hat.

"I'll take you."

"Okay. What happened to your hat, Mr. Jake?" His little finger reached out to trace a crease B.J.'s truck had pressed into it.

"Um, it got run over, Toby. Looks kind of bad, doesn't it?" Jake asked, but he looked at B.J. Sudden recognition appeared in her eyes, and she stared at his hat.

"I like your hat. When I grow up, I'm going to have one just like it."

"Don't you have a hat now?" Jake asked, an idea forming in his head.

"I have a baseball cap, but I don't have a cowboy hat."

"Toby, I think we'd better go," B.J. snapped, as if she were angry with her son.

"Wait a minute, B.J.," Jake said, stopping her. "I've got an idea. Why don't the three of us go hat shopping this afternoon? I'll get me a new one, and Toby could pick out a hat for his birthday. Would you like a hat as your birthday gift from me?"

"I can't go this afternoon," she immediately said.

Jake didn't know if she didn't want him to buy Toby a hat or if she was genuinely busy, but he wasn't going to give up. "How about tomorrow afternoon?"

"Please, Mommy?" Toby added.

Jake almost burst out laughing. If he'd asked B.J. to go shopping, just the two of them, he knew she would've turned him down flat. But when it involved Toby, her determination wavered.

"There's no need for you to buy him a hat, Jake."

Toby's face fell, and he hugged the boy closer to

him. "I want to buy him a present he'll enjoy. A hat's a lot more practical than a toy truck."

Suddenly she capitulated. "Fine. Tomorrow."

"Great. What time do you get out of school, Toby?"

"At lunchtime. What time is that, Mommy?"

"Twelve o'clock. But there's no need to interrupt your day, Jake. We can meet you some place in town at four," B.J. suggested.

"That's no problem. Why don't you and I meet here at eleven-thirty, drive to town and pick up Toby and have lunch at the sandwich shop? Then we'll go shopping."

"That's not necessary. You've got lots to do and—"

"Everyone's been riding me about not ever taking time off. If I want the afternoon off, then I'll take it. See you then." He set Toby on the ground and then leaned over to kiss her, briefly this time. It wasn't nearly as exciting as their earlier kiss, nor as satisfying, but it beat nothing at all.

Before she could protest or change their plans, he left the barn. He strode over to the indoor arena, figuring to check on the hands working there. As he opened the door, he heard Toby's little voice shouting a goodbye. He turned to wave at the pair.

B.J. didn't respond.

But the thought of the next afternoon kept a smile on Jake's face all day. He was pleased to have found such a good gift for Toby. Heck, the kid had lived on the ranch almost a year. He needed a cowboy hat.

Maybe some chaps, too. And a good pair of leather gloves. After all, he'd probably grow up and work on the ranch during his teen years for spending money. Might as well equip him right.

"Hey, Jake," Brett called to him as he was heading into the house that evening.

He turned around to await Brett. A feeling of satisfaction filled him. A good day's work, a good meal awaiting him and a lot to look forward to.

"You look mighty pleased with yourself," Brett commented, watching him as he stepped onto the porch.

"Yeah," Jake agreed with a grin. "It was a good day."

"Great. Uh, is it okay if I take tomorrow off? Anna and I thought we'd spend it together."

"If you don't mind, why not wait until Wednesday? I've got plans for tomorrow afternoon, and we don't want to leave the place too shorthanded."

Jake opened the door and strolled into the kitchen, knowing Brett would follow.

"Plans? What are you doing?"

"Birthday shopping with Toby."

The rest of the family was already in the kitchen, and Jake's words stopped all conversation. Suddenly everyone was staring at him.

"What?" he demanded, frowning.

"Is B.J. going?" Anna asked.

"Of course she is. I'm buying Toby a cowboy hat, and we have to try them on, find one that suits him." He ignored his family's intense interest. "I'm going to clean up. I won't be long."

"Take your time," Red said.

Once Jake was out the door, everyone started talking about his announcement.

"I wonder when he and B.J. decided this? Last night?" Janie asked.

"Probably this morning," Red said.

"This morning? When did he see B.J. this morning?" Pete asked, frowning.

"When he left you, he went straight to B.J.'s house, then the two of them walked over to the barn," Red reported, continuing to work at the kitchen cabinet, pouring green beans into a serving bowl.

"You spying on Jake?" Chad asked.

"Nope. Just working here at the sink, looking out the window. Couldn't help but see."

"Great," Janie said, enthusiastically. "Let us know if you see anything else."

JAKE STRODE from the house after dinner, wanting to check some supplies before he went into town the next day. Movement out of the corner of his eye caught his attention.

He turned toward B.J.'s house and saw what had distracted him. Toby.

His smile broadened. In Toby's hands was the rope he'd given him last week to practice.

"Hold still, Spot," Toby called to his dog as he swung the rope.

Jake realized he'd neglected an important detail in his roping instructions.

"Hey, Toby, how's it going?"

"Mr. Jake! Look! I've been practicing."

"I can see." Jack squatted down and scratched behind Spot's ears after the puppy wriggled his way to Jake. "But I forgot to tell you something."

"What, Mr. Jake?" the little boy said, raising his gaze anxiously. "I'm holding it just like you said."

Jake couldn't resist giving the boy a hug. He'd enjoyed teaching Toby to rope last week. The boy's serious concentration, emphasized by a frown on his forehead, had tickled him.

"You're doin' fine. But I forgot to mention that you shouldn't use Spot as a target. You might hurt him."

Toby's eyes widened in alarm. "Oh, no!" He reached for his dog, clutching him to his chest. "I wouldn't hurt Spot, Mr. Jake."

"I know you wouldn't. How about we set up a post over there—" he gestured toward the barn "—and you can practice on it? Then, when you've got it down, we'll take you out and let you try to rope a real cow."

Toby's eyes widened again, this time in excitement. "Gee, Mr. Jake, that'd be neat! I'll practice all the time!"

"But not tomorrow. We're going shopping for a hat, remember?"

"I remember. I want a hat just like yours."

"Not like this one," Jake said, fingering his cowboy hat. He forgot Toby as he remembered how his hat had been flattened. And the kiss that had preceded it. B. J. Anderson was some kisser.

"Mr. Jake?" Toby tugged on his jacket. "Why are you smiling?"

Jake stared at the boy, trying to collect his thoughts. "Uh, I guess I was thinking about your mom."

"Mommy?" Toby paused and then said, "Do you like my mommy?"

"Of course I do." Jake's mind flashed back to his previous thoughts. Yeah, he liked Toby's mother. B.J. was a very attractive woman.

"I like you teaching me things. Mommy doesn't know how to rope." Toby leaned against his knee, and Jake put his arm around him.

"You've got a good mom, but there are some things that only guys know about."

"Yeah," Toby agreed. Then, with some hesitation, he continued, "Can I ask you a question?"

"Sure, Toby. You can ask me anything."

"What's a ho?"

Jake frowned. "Well, it's a tool for digging in a garden."

"Oh."

"Why, Toby? Are you planning on planting a garden?'' Not that there was anything wrong with putting in a garden, but cowboys weren't farmers, and he'd thought Toby wanted to learn to be a cowboy.

"No. But when one of the boys at school called a girl that, our teacher made him go to time-out and told us not never to say it 'cause it was naughty.'' Toby's voice sounded puzzled.

Jake could understand his confusion. "Sorry, Toby, but I thought you meant a different word. The word you're asking about *is* bad. Your teacher was right.''

"But what does it mean?''

Jake was tempted to tell Toby to ask his mother. But he couldn't do that. "Uh, it's a name men call women when they think they're too—too friendly with other men. But a gentleman doesn't use it, and he wouldn't let anyone else use it if they're talking about his woman. I mean, his friend.''

"He'd punch him in the nose!'' Toby said with relish, his eyes lighting up.

"Yeah,'' Jake agreed. "And don't ever use that word yourself.''

"No, I won't.'' Toby put his hand on Jake's cheek. "Mr. Jake, if someone called my mommy that word, would you hit him?''

"Is that who they were talking about?'' Jake demanded, surprising emotion filling him.

"No. But if someone did, would you hit him?''

"Yeah, I would,'' Jake admitted. "I'd flatten him before he knew what hit him.'' He realized his hold on Toby had tightened, and he forced himself to relax.

Then he thought about what he'd just said. Maybe that hadn't been the best response to give an impressionable child.

He tried again. "Uh, Toby, fighting in school isn't a good idea, you know."

"I know, Mr. Jake. Our teacher told us."

"Great. Well, I've got to go check on some things."

"I have to go take my bath. Mommy makes me," Toby said in disgusted tones.

"That's what moms are for, Toby. Besides, ladies like us to smell good."

"Do you take lots of baths, Mr. Jake?"

"Well, usuallly I take showers, but, yeah, I take my fair share of them."

With a resigned shrug, Toby replied, "Okay, then I won't complain."

"Good boy," Jake said as he stood, patting Toby on the head.

"Mr. Jake?"

"Yeah?"

"If I have any more questions I can't ask Mommy, can I ask you?"

Jake grinned. He kind of liked playing the role of mentor to the four-year-old. He only hoped B.J. wouldn't mind. "Sure, Toby. Any time."

The two parted, and Jake headed toward the barn with a smile on his lips.

Chapter Nine

B.J. had changed her mind the next day, deciding going into town with Jake wasn't a good idea. When she tried to persuade him to her way of thinking, however, she met with solid resistance.

"No way. You're just trying to steal my idea for a present, but I thought of it first."

"Jake, that's not it. You can buy him a hat, but I don't think our appearing in town together is a good idea."

"Why not?"

"We're just trying to convince Red and Mildred, not the entire community. You know how fast gossip spreads around town."

"It doesn't matter."

B.J. crossed her arms and gave him an exasperated look.

"If you don't want to go, fine. I'll pick Toby up from school, and we'll go without you," Jake said, a stubborn look on his face.

"No, you're not going without me," she protested,

unable to face remaining at home while Jake took Toby.

"Then let's go."

She did as he said, but she wasn't happy about it. They had a silent ride into town.

Any tension was dispelled as soon as Toby saw them waiting. He broke into a run, his face beaming.

"Now, aren't you glad we didn't cancel?" Jake murmured.

B.J. shot him an irritated look, but he was right. She hated disappointing her son. She knelt for Toby's hug and was surprised to discover Jake beside her. After Toby hugged her, Jake held out his arms.

"I should get a hug, too, shouldn't I?"

Toby didn't hesitate, but B.J. stood, her heart churning. Toby already had put Jake on a pedestal. How much was their pretense going to hurt her son?

"Mrs. Anderson?"

She turned to see Toby's preschool teacher coming toward her. "Hello, Mrs. Bell. How are things going?"

"Just lovely. I wanted to be sure that Toby found you. He told me he was supposed to meet you and Jake today instead of taking the bus."

Jake stood with Toby's arms around his neck. "Mornin', Loretta."

"Mornin', Jake. I see Toby found his hero. You're all he's talked about all morning."

"Must've been a pretty dull morning, then," Jake returned with a laugh.

B.J. sighed. Mrs. Bell was approaching retirement, but she could no more resist Jake Randall's charm than any other woman. The teacher laughed and reached out to touch Jake's arm. "You've been good for Toby. Now when the other boys talk about their daddies, he always mentions you."

B.J. froze, dismay filling her. "You never mentioned a problem, Mrs. Bell."

The woman's gaze flew from Jake's to hers. "Oh, there isn't a problem, Mrs. Anderson. At least not one that you could help. Toby sometimes felt a little left out because he only has one parent. He's not the only one with that problem."

B.J. had known, once Toby started school, that he would feel the loss of his father. But she hadn't planned on Jake being the substitute. "I hope you will remind him that Jake is a friend, not—not his father."

Very gently, with a sympathetic smile, Mrs. Bell said, "Toby doesn't get confused, Mrs. Anderson. He's a very smart little boy."

B.J. nodded and avoided Jake's gaze. "Thank you for checking on Toby, Mrs. Bell. He's enjoying your class very much."

They said their goodbyes and got into Jake's truck, Toby between them. Jake helped him fasten his seat belt before B.J. remembered. Her mind was too occupied with Toby's teacher's words.

"Quit worryin'," Jake said softly over Toby's head.

Her gaze met his, but she couldn't respond. Not

worry? About her only child and how she might be hurting him? Nothing could keep her from doing that.

"I told everyone about my birthday present," Toby announced brightly. Then a shadow fell across his face. "But Larry said I shouldn't tell. That it had to be a secret. Does it have to be a secret, Mr. Jake?"

"No, Toby. I'll get you something else as a secret. Then—"

"No!" B.J. protested. "No, Jake, only one present. You'll spoil Toby if you're not careful."

"Are you only going to buy him one present?" Jake challenged, squaring his jaw and staring at her.

"That has nothing to do with it. I'm his mother." And Jake Randall wasn't his father. She had to make that point, even if she didn't say it out loud.

Instead of responding, Jake put the truck in gear and headed toward the main street of Rawhide. "Are you hungry, Toby?"

"Yeah! We had juice and cookies, but I dropped one of mine on the floor and it broke into little pieces. Mrs. Bell wouldn't let me eat it."

"Thank goodness," B.J. said with a laugh, reaching over to push back his hair, which always flopped onto his forehead. "I think you're about due for a haircut."

"Hey, me too. How about we get our hair cut before we buy our hats, Toby?"

B.J. bit her bottom lip. Toby was still a little leery of barbershops. Until a few months ago, she or Mildred had usually trimmed his hair. But when Mr. Jake suggested something, Toby, it appeared, had no doubts.

She was going to have to get the man to recommend baths. Though she had to admit Toby had been amazingly compliant last night.

"Yeah, that'd be fun," Toby agreed.

"Okay with you, Mom?" Jake asked, surprising her with the familiar term.

"Yes, of course, if Toby doesn't mind."

"That way our hats will fit better, right, Toby?"

"Right, Mr. Jake."

Lunch was a revelation to B.J. All her admonitions to Toby about manners seldom had taken hold in his consciousness. But today, when Jake took his napkin and spread it across his lap, Toby immediately did the same. When Jake said thank-you to the waitress, Toby did also.

Of course, Jake's words had the young woman blushing and batting her eyelashes. Toby's earned him a pat on the head.

"So, what'll you have, Toby?" Jake asked.

"What are you having?" Toby asked.

Jake looked over the top of the menu, sharing his amusement with B.J. She supposed, if her son was going to have a hero, Jake Randall wasn't a bad choice. But she was worried about how far the hero worship would go. Even so, she smiled at Jake.

"I'm thinking of having a big, fat, juicy hamburger."

"Me, too."

Surprise, surprise, surprise.

"B.J.? You made up your mind yet?"

She turned her attention to the menu instead of the two males at the table and quickly made a decision. "Yes, I'll have the chicken-salad sandwich."

"Humph! Girl food," Jake said with a teasing grin.

"Yeah, girl food," Toby agreed.

This hero worship could get tiresome.

"I am a girl, after all," she contended.

"The prettiest one I've ever seen," Jake said, his grin widening.

"Yeah, you're pretty, Mommy," Toby seconded.

Maybe she could stand Toby agreeing with Jake after all.

The next stop was the barbershop. Al, who had cut Jake's hair since he was a little boy, trimmed first his hair and then Toby's, following Toby's directions to cut his hair just like Mr. Jake's.

B.J. sat along the wall, watching the three of them as they indulged in man talk, feeling a little excluded. It was a new experience for her. She and Mildred had formed Toby's world for almost all his life. She wasn't used to sharing him.

She thought again about what Mrs. Bell had said. She'd have to have a talk with Toby, make sure he understood that Jake was a friend.

Jake insisted on paying for Toby's haircut. B.J. would've argued more, but she didn't want to draw attention to Jake's action. Looked as though she needed to have a talk with Jake, as well as Toby.

"All right, let's go buy us a couple of hats, Toby my boy," Jake said, grinning at first Toby and then B.J. He seemed to be enjoying his afternoon in town.

He grabbed Toby's hand and then, to B.J.'s surprise, reached back for hers. "Come on, B.J. You're not feeling left out, are you, 'cause you didn't get a haircut?"

"No, I'll get one later."

He came to an abrupt halt. "You're going to get your hair cut? I was just teasing. I don't think—"

"Trimmed, Jake. I'm going to get my hair trimmed. I'm not going to cut it short, because it takes too much time to style a short hairstyle."

Toby apparently felt left out, because he turned in front of Jake, still holding his hand. "I like Mommy's hair. Sometimes she lets me brush it."

"You've got good taste, Toby. Do you think she'd let me brush it?" His gaze left her son to stare at her hair.

"Jake!" she protested. Somehow the picture of Jake brushing her hair, feeling his hands slipping through the long strands, sensing his big, warm, hard body near hers, stirred her more than the compliments he'd paid her.

He grinned and leaned down for a quick kiss before she could protest. "And that doesn't count for the one you tricked me out of," he muttered as he started walking again, pulling her and Toby along with him to the store two doors down.

"Why not?"

"You know why. Here we are, Toby." He held the door open for Toby and then her.

"Hey, Jake, haven't seen you in a coon's age," Harvey Holmes greeted him. "And you brought along Miz Anderson and her boy. How you folks doing?"

Fortunately the store was almost empty, since B.J. figured no one would've missed Harvey's booming voice.

Harvey showed them to the hats and left them alone to make their selections, promising to help if they had any questions.

"Aunt Mildred said the good guys always wear white hats," Toby said, studying his choices.

"In the movies, they do, but that's because they don't have to worry about them looking clean." Jake was studying the different colors and styles seriously.

B.J. saw one that looked Toby's size and picked it up. The Resistol brand was a good one, she knew, but she had no idea how much the price would be. With a gasp, she put the hat back down. "Jake," she whispered, moving closer to him.

"Yeah, honey?" he answered in a distracted fashion.

"Jake, these hats are too expensive."

He gave her a surprised look. "I always buy Resistols."

"It doesn't matter what you buy. I'm talking about for Toby. They have some hats at the grocery store that will do just fine for him." She turned to explain to her son, but Jake grabbed her arm.

"You buy him all the hats you want at the grocery store, but *I'm* buying him a Resistol. He needs to learn about quality. This hat'll last him for years." His jaw was squared again, a sure sign that he had the bit in his teeth.

"The hat will last, but Toby'll outgrow it in a year."

"Great. I'll know what to get him next year," he said calmly, and took a hat, quite similar to the one she'd flattened, off the wall and set it on his head. "What do you think, Toby?"

"That looks like your old hat," the boy said, staring up at him, studying the hat from several different angles.

"Yeah, it does, doesn't it? I don't change my mind much," he admitted with another grin. "Which one do you like?"

Unerringly Toby selected a miniature version of the dark gray hat Jake was wearing. "I like this one."

Jake led him over to a mirror and set the hat on the little boy's head, squatting down beside him to compare the hats. "Hey, we look just alike, don't we?"

Toby made an adjustment in the angle of his hat so it more correctly reflected Jake's and sighed with pleasure. "Yeah, just alike. Right, Mommy?"

Their satisfaction with what they saw in the mirror would've been humorous if B.J. weren't filled with worry. But she smiled at Toby, agreeing that he and Mr. Jake were almost twins.

In truth, they did look alike, even without the hats. They both had dark hair and a similar build. Her husband had been tall, even if he hadn't shown the muscle Jake had. He'd been a law student when they met, spending his days indoors.

"You folks found what you need?" Harvey asked, approaching them again.

"I believe we have. Toby and I like these."

"I'm not surprised. You've bought the same hat since you were a boy, Jake. Starting Toby off right, I see."

"Yeah. And pretty soon I'll be buying hats for the twins, too." A satisfied smile crossed his lips.

"I'd better lay in some smaller sizes, the way the Randall clan is growing," Harvey said with a laugh. The sly look he sent B.J.'s way wasn't missed by Jake. He turned to her, too.

"How about you, B.J.?" he suddenly asked.

"What?" she asked, looking up from Toby, who was staring at himself and Jake in the mirror.

"You need a hat?"

"No, it's not my birthday. That's why Jake is buying Toby a present, Mr. Holmes. It's his birthday."

"Make it Harvey. We're not formal here. So, it's your birthday, young man?"

"In a few days. The twenty-seventh, the same day as Mr. Jake's," Toby said proudly, as if he'd planned his arrival on such an important day.

"Yeah, we're twins," Jake said with a wink to the store owner.

"I can see the resemblance," Harvey agreed solemnly, putting an extra shine on Toby's grin. "Come on over here, and I'll ring you up."

They were almost finished with their purchase, with B.J. reminding herself to discuss money with Jake, when the door opened, the bell above announcing a new arrival.

They all looked up, but Jake was the only one who recognized the man who arrived.

"Butch Gardner!" he exclaimed, and left the counter to greet the man with his hand out.

"Jake!" the man returned, pumping Jake's hand with pleasure. The two men exchanged greetings and questioned each other about what had happened the past few years. It seemed Butch, who'd lived near Rawhide most of his early years, was returning to town.

After the first wave of words had passed, the man looked past Jake and saw B.J. and Toby waiting for him. Jake turned, too, and B.J. assumed he intended to introduce them, but before he could, Butch spoke.

"Jake, you old sneak. You've done gone and got yourself that son you always wanted! And a beautiful wife, to boot. Congratulations, man."

There was a moment of silence when B.J.'s alarmed look met Jake's. She didn't want to look at Toby. She opened her mouth to correct the man, but Jake beat her to it.

"Sorry, Butch, but you're wrong on both counts. Toby is B. J. Anderson's son, and neither of them belongs to me." Jake's easy smile relieved some of Butch's embarrassment.

"Sorry, ma'am. It's an old habit of mine, leaping to conclusions. Hope I didn't offend you." He doffed his black hat as he apologized.

"No, of course not." She put her hand on Toby's shoulder. "Shall we wait for you out in the pickup, Jake?"

"No, we won't be a minute," Jake assured her before he turned back to his friend. "You'll have to come out to the place, Butch, and see everyone. All three of the others are married now, and Pete has two sons."

"No kidding? Man, I didn't think any of you would ever try marriage again. And two boys? Then the Randall ranch is safe for the next generation? That was always your concern," Butch reminded him.

Harvey laughed. "Everyone knows how worried Jake was about not having any kids. He didn't want different blood taking over at the Randalls'."

Different blood. B.J. turned that phrase over in her head. Apparently Jake was big on bloodlines. He'd talked about that at their dinner in Wyndom, how thrilled he was to have the next generation of real Randalls. B.J. didn't need a sack of grain to hit her in the head. She got the point.

"Nope, no problem now. There'll be Randalls on the place for a long time," Jake said, his grin even broader. "We've got to go, but the family's having a party for Halloween. Where shall we send the invite?''

''Mrs. Potter's putting me up at her bed and breakfast until I get settled some place.''

''You looking for a job? We could use someone right now,'' Jake said, as if he'd suddenly realized his friend might be looking for work.

''I don't need any pity hiring, Jake,'' Butch said, squaring his jaw.

''Man, with all we've had going on, none of us puts in a full week anymore. And Lefty died last winter, before Christmas. We've never replaced him.''

''Lefty? That's too bad. But are you sure you need someone? 'Cause I can—''

''Jake's been asking for most of the year, Butch,'' Harvey said. ''There's not a lot of good help around.''

Jake shot the store owner a grateful look. Then he quickly worked out the details with his friend before sweeping B.J. and Toby out the door.

Once they were in the truck, B.J. started to ask Jake about the man, but Toby had another question in mind.

''Why can't I be your little boy, Mr. Jake? Is something wrong with my blood?''

Chapter Ten

B.J. sucked in a deep breath.

Jake spoke before she could think of what to say.

"Nah. There's nothing wrong with your blood, Toby. They just meant we're not kin to each other. You know, like you and your mom."

"Oh."

B.J. desperately sought a change of subject. "How did you do in school today, Toby? Did you learn to write any new words?"

Her little boy turned and frowned at her, his look distracted. "Mm-hmm. Mr. Jake?"

"Yes, Toby?"

"How—?"

"Toby, did you know the Randalls are having a Halloween party?" B.J. asked, hoping to distract him again. She didn't think it would be a good idea to pursue the idea of Toby being Jake's son.

This time she was more successful.

"A Halloween party? With masks and everything?" Toby demanded. "Can we go?"

"It's bad manners to invite yourself to a party," she gently reminded him.

"Don't worry about it, Toby," Jake assured him. "Of course you're invited. And you can wear a mask."

"I'm going to be a monster!" Toby assured his hero. "Right, Mommy?"

"We'll see," she said, offering a mother's standard fare.

"You won't scare me, will you?" Jake asked, pretending to shake in fear.

"Nah," Toby replied, imitating Jake's way of answering. "'Sides, you wouldn't be scared. Maybe Mommy would." Toby cut his gaze toward his mother, a grin on his face.

B.J. was willing to play along, as long as it kept her son happy. "I just might be. Promise you'll tell me it's you?"

"Yeah, Mommy."

"And if she gets scared, I'll comfort her," Jake added, and shot a teasing look at B.J.

The thought of Jake's big arms wrapped around her, his hands stroking her, sent shivers through her body. His brown eyes caressed her over Toby's head, and she broke away from his gaze.

"I won't scare you, Mommy," her son promised.

"Doggone it, Toby, why'd you promise that? I was going to get to hug your mom."

"I saw Bobby's mommy hugging."

B.J. frowned, unable to follow her son's comment. Before she could ask about his words, Jake did.

"Was she happy about it?"

"Uh-huh. She was hugging Bobby's new daddy."

"Good for her," Jake said, smiling at B.J. over Toby's head.

"Yeah. Bobby says he's his real daddy. But they don't have the same blood. Do they?"

"Probably not," Jake agreed.

"Then how come he's his real daddy?"

B.J. could think of nothing to derail the conversation. Even the subject of Toby's monster costume probably wouldn't distract him.

"Because his mom married the man. That would make him his daddy."

"Even if they don't have the same blood?"

"Well, he wouldn't be his *real* daddy, but he'd be his stepdaddy."

"Oh."

B.J. decided the all-male conversation had gone on long enough. "Did you tell Jake that Aunt Mildred is making cupcakes for the class for your birthday?" she asked. "And that she'll make one for Jake, too?"

"No. Do you like chocolate cupcakes, Mr. Jake?"

"You bet. I'll be looking forward to one of your cupcakes. Maybe I could come over and eat it for breakfast."

"Yeah!"

B.J. breathed a sigh of relief. At least Toby didn't

seem upset about anything. She took a deep breath and leaned back against the seat.

Then Toby calmly announced, "Bobby said he thought I was going to have a new daddy."

B.J. felt the blood drain out of her head. She was so shocked, she didn't realize Jake had slammed on the brakes until he'd stopped the truck on the side of the road.

"What are you talking about?" he demanded harshly.

B.J.'s arm immediately went around her son's shoulders. She didn't want anyone speaking so cruelly to her little boy, but she knew how devastated Toby would be to find his hero unhappy with him. "Jake—" she began.

"Why did Bobby say that?" Jake ignored her warning.

"I told him about you kissing Mommy, and he said that's what his new daddy always did." Toby squared his shoulders and lifted his chin to stare at Jake. "Are you mad?"

B.J. didn't realize she was holding her breath until Jake expelled his own.

"No, son, I'm not angry. But Bobby was wrong. Men and women kiss without getting married. You know, I've been married before, and I don't intend to marry. Your mom and I were just being friendly."

Friendly. Of course, that was the correct explanation. She was glad he'd done away with poor Toby's dreams. If he hadn't, Toby might have really been hurt.

"Never?" Toby whispered.

"No, never."

Toby turned a troubled glance to B.J. "Is that okay, Mommy?"

"Of course, sweetie," she replied, swallowing inexplicable tears in the back of her throat. "I'm sorry if you're disappointed, but when Mildred marries Red, you'll have a grandpa. Then when they have— have things at school for daddies, Red can come with you."

"Sure. I like Mr. Red."

She'd never been so proud of her child. He was hurting inside. And it was her fault. She was going to have to tell Mildred the truth—and let Mildred make her own decision. But she couldn't hurt her son any more.

Hugging him closer to her, she leaned over and kissed the top of his head. "Mr. Red likes you, too. I think we should ask Mildred if you can walk her down the aisle when she marries Mr. Red."

While Toby, distracted again, excitedly asked B.J. what she meant, Jake pulled the truck back on the road and continued on to the ranch.

DAMN! HE HADN'T MEANT to hurt the kid's feelings. Jake looked sideways at the other two in the truck. They made a tender picture, mother and son, her arm around him.

If Jake were ever going to marry again, it would be to someone like B.J., warm, loving, caring.

If? What was he thinking? There was no question of him marrying! Never!

He glared at B.J. as if she were responsible for the shocking thought that had intruded into his head. It was those kisses of hers. The unexpected hunger he'd discovered for touching B. J. Anderson was the reason. For only a second, he considered being married to the woman beside him, having the right to touch her whenever he wanted.

Having her touch him.

He hurriedly sent those thoughts out the window, before his body could show the effects of the warmth that filled him. Lately he'd felt out of control too often.

By the time he'd parked the truck in its usual place, he'd concentrated his thoughts on more-mundane things and convinced himself everything was okay. He turned off the engine and turned to smile at his passengers. The sight of Toby whispering to his mother puzzled Jake.

"Everything all right?"

"Yes," B.J. said, giving Jake a brief look before turning back to her son. "It's all right, Toby. Just be sure you say thank-you."

"Thank you for my hat, Mr. Jake," Toby said. The serious look on his little face worried Jake.

"You're welcome. Happy birthday, pal. You like it, don't you?"

"Sure. It's just like yours." His smile this time wasn't his best, but Jake was pleased.

"Sweetie, run on over to the house and tell Mildred I'll be there in a minute. I need to talk to Mr. Jake." B.J. didn't look at Jake as she spoke, her gaze focused on her child.

But Jake felt anticipation build in him. Time alone with B.J. meant the possibility of a few more of those drugging kisses. He couldn't afford too many, but already his body was revving up with the thought of holding her again.

"See ya, Toby," he called out as the little boy slipped past his mother and out the door on her side. Toby waved but said nothing. Briefly Jake was distracted from thoughts of B.J. as he watched the child jog to their house, clutching the bag containing his new hat.

"Everything all right with Toby?"

"No," B.J. said, and he could hear icicles hanging off that one word.

"What's wrong?"

"We can't pretend any longer." She was staring straight ahead.

Jake studied her face, wishing she'd look at him. He was confused. "I thought we were talking about Toby."

"We are. Toby is believing our pretense. And I don't want him hurt."

"I told him we were just being friendly." In Jake's mind, his explanation would take care of the problem.

"It's not enough, Jake. Soon he'll hear rumors from other kids. Because—because it's what he wants, he'll ignore your explanation."

"What do you mean, it's what he wants?"

Now she looked at him, but her expression was a mixture of anger and disgust, and he almost wished she were staring straight ahead. "Come on, Jake. You must realize Toby has a bad case of hero worship. And since he's seen us..." She paused and Jake watched her swallow. He wanted to stroke her throat as he traced the movement with his gaze.

He leaned toward her, not even realizing it until she jerked away from him. Pulling himself together, he asked, "After he's seen us what?"

"Kissing! After he saw us in the barn, he obviously felt our—our relationship has changed."

"Yeah. We recognize each other now," Jake drawled at her obvious understatement.

"We always recognized each other," she said indignantly, looking at him again.

That indignation made her lips form a sexy pout that drew his lips like a magnet. But she only allowed a brief touching before she put her hands on his chest and pushed.

"Don't."

"Sorry. I couldn't help myself."

She glared at him.

"So what are you saying? Around Toby we don't pretend? I think that might be—"

"Impossible. That would be impossible. I'm saying

we shouldn't pretend anymore. At all." She pressed those lips tightly together.

"What about Mildred and Red?" He wanted to protest more, to tell her she couldn't stop what had already been set in motion. But he was afraid she'd question his motives. Red and Mildred were safer.

"I'm going to tell Mildred the truth."

Jake frowned. "Do you think that's fair? They've made plans." So had he. For a little more closeness with B.J.

"I won't risk my son's happiness."

"Aren't you being melodramatic? I'm not going to hurt Toby." He wouldn't do that. He and Toby were pals.

She lifted her chin. "No. Our pretense is over, Jake. You're on your own in the future."

"Hey, don't act like I begged you." His pride was hurt. She thought he couldn't manage on his own? He conveniently pushed aside that Friday night in Rawhide. *She* was the one who'd wanted to continue the charade.

"I know." Her words came out with defeat, and she sagged against the car seat. "I made a mistake. I'm sorry I asked you to do this—" she waved one hand distractedly "—and—and I hope you don't have any unpleasant repercussions from it."

"Hey, B.J., I don't have anything to complain about," he said softly, fighting the urge to gather her against him.

She shook her head no, her chin lowered. Before

he could think of anything else to say, she slid from the truck and hurried to her home.

Damn! That made two Andersons he'd upset this afternoon. He slapped the steering wheel, angry with himself and with the events of the day. Which had started off with such promise.

His original idea had been so simple.

A little friendliness to scare off scheming women.

But things had gotten complicated.

He threw himself from the truck, not wanting to think about what had happened. When he reached the kitchen, he didn't slow down, in spite of the fact that Red and his three sisters-in-law were there.

"Jake!" Janie called out. "How did the day go?"

"Fine! Damn fine! In fact, outstandingly damn fine!"

He realized he hadn't been as tactful as he'd intended when a stunned silence followed him from the room.

B.J. ENTERED THE HOUSE and squared her shoulders. She couldn't put off her talk with Mildred. It was going to be hard enough without time to think about it.

"Mildred?"

"In the kitchen," Mildred called back.

As B.J. entered the most popular room in the house, Toby was showing Mildred his hat.

"It's just like Mr. Jake's," he explained, but the

excitement that had earlier filled his voice wasn't there.

"That's a mighty fine hat. A fine birthday present." Mildred shot B.J. a puzzled look over Toby's head.

"Why don't you go find a place in your room to keep it so it won't get messed up, Toby. And then lie down for half an hour. You've had a big day."

"Aw, Mommy, I'm not tired," he protested.

"In half an hour, 'Popeye' will be on television. You can get up then and watch it."

After the little boy had left the kitchen, Mildred spoke first. "What's wrong with Toby? Did everything go all right?"

"No, it didn't." With a sigh, B.J. sank into one of the chairs around the breakfast table. "Sit down, Mildred."

When Mildred had joined her, B.J. said, "Jake and I aren't going to get married or have an affair or even be friends."

Her stark announcement didn't cause Mildred to fall over in a dead faint, which was good, but it didn't make her happy, either. "What do you mean?"

"I mean I've lied to you, Mildred. Jake and I were playing a game. At first we pretended because Jake didn't want Ceci chasing him around the restaurant, and I wanted to keep Bill Morris at bay. Then—" she drew a deep breath before continuing "—I wanted you to think that Jake and I were serious because I knew you would agree to marry Red."

Without another word, Mildred rose from the table and returned to the dinner preparations Toby had interrupted.

"Mildred? What are you going to do?"

"About what?"

"Red. You are still going to marry him, aren't you? Please don't give up your happiness. I don't need a man to take care of me. You know that." B.J. studied her aunt, her best friend, her biggest supporter, with pain in her heart.

"I don't know what I'm going to do. I have to talk to Red." She kept her back to B.J.

Getting up, B.J. crossed the room to Mildred's side, trying to get a glimpse of her face. "I'm sorry I lied to you. I thought I was helping you."

"I'm sorry, too. You and Jake seemed so right together."

"No. No, we're not."

"So what I saw on the front porch was an act?" Now Mildred looked at her, her eyes piercing in their intensity.

"Yes." She couldn't keep the blood from her cheeks, but she returned Mildred's gaze.

"You must be one whale of an actress."

Could her cheeks get even redder? B.J. wondered. "Jake's a very sexy man, Mildred. I'm not made of stone. But that doesn't mean—"

"Uh-uh. I know what that means."

B.J. closed her mouth. She did, too. It meant she'd have some lonely nights. She muttered "Sorry," and left the room. She *was* sorry. Because from now on, she was going to avoid Jake Randall if it was the last thing she did.

JAKE WATCHED the unloading of Pete's new purchase with a jaundiced eye. The gelding was reputed to be one of the meanest around, perfect for the rodeo circuit. He attempted to justify his reputation by flashing his teeth toward the cowboys who each held a rope tied around his neck. Then he lashed out with his back hooves, barely missing Pete.

"Damn it, Pete, I don't think you made a good buy."

Pete, a little breathless from his fast retreat, grinned at his brother. "Why not?"

"He's out of control."

"Nah. He's just mean and ornery."

"I think you should get rid of him," Jake insisted.

"Why? We're keeping *you* around." Pete's grin widened as Jake stared at him.

"What do you mean?"

"Since you spent the afternoon with B.J. and Toby, you've been in a worse mood than this horse could ever have. You've snapped everyone's head off. Janie was even fearful of letting you hold the twins, afraid you'd stand them in the corner for not drinking all their milk."

Jake stared at his brother, shock filling him. "I haven't— I mean, I wouldn't ever do anything to—

Janie didn't say that!'' he finished indignantly, reading the teasing laughter in his brother's eyes.

"Nope, she didn't. But she might.''

"No, she wouldn't. I've been in a bad mood lately, that's all. There's lots of headaches on a ranch.''

"Yeah. And the only time they bothered me was when Janie had left me.'' Pete leveled a look at Jake that spoke volumes.

Jake didn't want to have a discussion, out loud or with stares, about women. Women had no place in his life. He was lucky to escape that little game he'd played with B.J. with no problems.

That's what he kept telling himself. He was lucky. He didn't have any interest in women. Especially B.J.

And his heart told him he was a liar.

"No one left me, brother. Got that? If I've been short with anyone lately, it's because my mind has been on—on the rising feed prices.''

"Yeah, right,'' Pete agreed, but the sarcasm in his voice indicated the opposite. Before Jake could protest again, Pete turned to one of the cowboys standing watching the horse struggle against his captors and ordered, "Go see if B.J. is here.''

Jake felt his gut clench. He hadn't seen her in a week. He'd looked for her, waited for her, but he hadn't seen her. Anticipation began building. It was ridiculous that they never saw each other when they lived only a few yards apart. "B.J.'s coming?'' He tried to keep his words casual.

"Yeah. She's going to check out Testosterone, see if he's healthy."

"That's a damn odd name for a— What?" Jake roared as the realization sat in. "You're going to put B.J. in a pen with that monster?"

"I think the name is quite appropriate," a sexy voice said behind him.

Jake spun around to discover B.J. watching him. As soon as they made eye contact, she shifted to Pete. "I'm here. Are you ready for me?"

Jake's gaze hungrily traveled over her. She didn't look any different than he remembered. Sexy as hell in her jeans. She was wearing a denim jacket to protect her against the crispness in the air. Her hair was braided as usual, with dark wisps that had escaped to frame her beautiful face.

"Hey, B.J.," someone called, and she looked away. Lifting a hand, she acknowledged Butch Gardner.

He trotted over, an admiring look on his face.

Jake frowned. Shortly after Butch had arrived on the ranch, he'd questioned Jake about B.J. Jake regretted now that he'd told his friend B.J. wasn't his woman.

"I enjoyed last night," Butch said, a big smile on his face.

Jake caught Pete's sharp look at him, but he ignored it. "Last night?"

"Yeah. I ran into B.J. and her aunt and boy at the

steak house, and they invited me to join them," Butch said, but his gaze never left B.J.'s face.

"Yes, it was fun," she said, but purposely turned her attention back to Pete. "I'm ready to check out your new star."

"Great. We'll put him—"

"No! You most certainly will not!" Jake roared. "You're not getting anywhere near that monster."

Chapter Eleven

Even the cantankerous horse came to a standstill at Jake's protest. Certainly the cowboys gathered around stared at him, including Pete and Butch.

B.J., however, was determined to minimize the embarrassment. "Don't be silly, Jake. Surely you approve of my work, if nothing else." With a stiff smile, she turned toward the animal.

A powerful hand clamped down on her arm. "I meant what I said. You're not getting close to that horse." This time his voice was low, quiet...and as hard as steel.

B.J. stared down at his hand. She'd missed him this past week, had dreamed of seeing him again, having him touch her. But not like this. "I don't think my doing my job has anything to do with you. Pete is the one who asked me to come."

Jake faced his brother, but he didn't turn loose of her. "Pete?"

"Jake, I wouldn't let B.J. get hurt. We're going to—" He broke off and stared first at B.J., then Jake.

Finally he looked at B.J. again. "Hell, I'm sorry, B.J. Bill me for the time."

B.J. stared, openmouthed at the two Randall brothers. She and Pete had worked well together in the past. Now, like Jake, he was losing faith in her? "Do you realize that I can't sign the health certificate if I don't examine him?" She didn't have to add that Pete couldn't send the animal to any rodeos without the certificate. Pete knew that.

Pete shifted his weight, clearly uneasy. "I'll get him checked out at one of the rodeos. There are always vets hanging around."

"And waste the space in the truck if he's not okay? And what about your sale? Wouldn't it be too late to return him if you wait until then?"

"If the horse is no good, I'll personally make up the difference," Jake promised, nodding at his brother.

B.J. wrenched her arm from Jake's hold, taking him by surprise, and faced him. "Why don't you just come out and say what you're thinking? I can't handle my work because I'm a woman!"

"You know I think you're good at what you do. But this horse is a mean one. I don't want you hurt...on Randall property."

"Afraid I'll sue? I absolve you of all responsibility. Did everyone hear that?" she asked, looking at their audience, which was paying rapt attention. She received a few nods. "See, Jake, you're home free."

She whirled around, ready to go to work, but Jake seized hold of her again.

"We'll be back in a minute," Jake muttered to his brother, and started off in the direction of the nearest building, pulling her behind him.

"Jake Randall, turn loose of me!" she protested, but those words didn't stop her progress. When she dug in her heels, he turned to look her in the eye.

The expression on his face told her he wasn't going to give in easily, but it didn't prepare her for what followed. Without saying another word, he slung her over his shoulder and turned back to the barn.

Stunned by the suddenness of his move, it took B.J. a little time to compose herself, if that was possible hanging upside down staring at his rear end.

"Jake Randall! Put me down!" she protested, trying to keep her voice down, hoping to draw less attention to the pair of them. Then she thought about the ridiculousness of that idea. Everyone on the ranch was watching them!

She got no response from Jake. Pushing against his back, she tried kicking him, but he held her legs tightly against his chest. "Jake!" she protested again.

He ignored her and opened the barn door.

Inside, he slammed the door shut and then dumped her on her feet. She almost lost her balance but quickly recovered, outrage stiffening her spine.

"How dare you, Jake Randall! You've embarrassed me in front of the entire ranch!"

"Better to embarrass you than to let your skull get cracked open with a vicious kick from that horse."

His grim words should have invited thanks, she supposed, but he wasn't about to get off that easy. "All you've done is tell everyone you have no faith in me as a veterinarian. And it's because I'm a woman!"

"Don't start that sexist crap, B.J. That horse is dangerous." He stood there, his hands on his hips, a righteous expression on his face.

"Then why are you letting the cowboys deal with that horse if he's so dangerous?" She put her hands on her hips, matching his stance. Let him get out of this one if he could.

"Because—because they're used to dealing with difficult animals." The righteous expression had fled, replaced by some uneasiness.

"And as a vet, I'm used to dealing with what, exactly? Kindergartners?"

"Don't be sarcastic!"

"What do you expect me to be? You've made me look like an idiot!"

"I'm trying to protect you!" He paused and then added, "For Toby's sake. He doesn't have a father. Do you want him to be without his mother, too?" He stopped and put his hands back on his hips, again sounding righteous.

"You think I can't check out that horse without being hurt? For heaven's sake, we're going to put him in a chute and tranquilize him. Did you think I was going to walk up and let him kick me from here to Cheyenne?'' She imitated his stance, taking a step forward this time, tossing her braid over her shoulder.

"Okay, okay, so you've got a good plan. But you could still get hurt."

"So could you, every day. I could get hurt driving down the road. Anyone could. But you don't stop doing your job, and I'm not going to stop doing mine. Unless you refuse to use my services anymore.'' She paused and prayed he wouldn't go that far. "If you do that, I'll have to leave. Because no one else will hire me if the Randalls won't.''

She wasn't sure how long they stared at each other, only a couple of feet between them. With her chin raised in challenge, she couldn't look away. But he didn't look away, either, frowning at her, studying her. When he finally spoke, it wasn't about the horse.

"Damn, I want to kiss you."

"Jake!" she protested. She'd been holding her breath for his cooperation, and all he could think about was kissing.

"How's Toby?" he finally asked.

She shook her head, trying to follow the disjointed conversation. "He's fine."

"I haven't seen him since we went shopping for his hat. Has he been wearing it?"

"No, he thought he should wait until his birthday." She didn't want to tell Jake how upset Toby had been that Jake could never be his daddy. She and her son had had a long talk about Jake Randall. She thought Toby understood now.

"Doesn't he like it?"

"Of course he does. He'll wear it in two days." She bit her bottom lip, worrying about what he'd say next.

He stepped closer and rubbed his thumb across her bottom lip.

She gasped and pulled her head back. Anything to break contact with his powerful touch. "We—we can't do that, Jake."

"Yeah, but—"

"Jake?" Pete called through the door. "Everything all right in there?"

B.J. felt the heat flame her cheeks as she realized half the ranch had been waiting outside the barn door to see what would happen. "Oh, no! Jake! Everyone's been waiting, thinking— Who knows what they're thinking. You've got to let me inspect the horse, or I'll be ruined!"

"You're being too dramatic," he protested, but she read comprehension in his eyes. "Come on," he growled, and turned to unbolt the door.

Pete moved back abruptly, almost as if he'd been listening. Over his shoulder, B.J. could see all the cowhands staring at them. She closed her eyes briefly and then tried to look cheerful.

Moving past Jake, she nodded to Pete. "Well, let's get that ornery horse in a chute. I've got other animals to see when I finish here."

"Jake?" Pete asked, looking over her shoulder.

"Yeah, it's okay. She explained what she was going to do."

B.J. pasted a smile on her face. "His majesty has decided I know my business after all." She walked over to the cowboys holding the horse, their ropes taut.

"You'd better get him in a chute before your arms give out," she recommended. "Or before Jake changes his mind."

One of the cowboys grinned. "Aw, you can't blame him, B.J. A woman as pretty as you, it'd be a shame to leave any scars."

She glared at him. As she turned away, she caught a curious stare from Butch. He didn't return her smile. Instead, he walked over to Jake.

She turned her attention to the horse. She'd made up her mind she was only going to concentrate on animals. She didn't want anything to do with cowboys, even one as nice as Butch.

And some of them, not to name names, could be as ornery as that horse. And just as hard to understand.

"I THOUGHT YOU SAID there was nothing between you and B.J.," Butch said in a low voice.

Jake, watching every move B.J. made, his mind concentrating on her safety, scarcely heard him. "Hmm?"

"Did you two have a fight? Is that why you told me she wasn't your woman?" Butch persisted.

Jake jerked around as Butch's questions finally penetrated his head. "Why do you say that?"

Butch gave him a look of disgust. "Because you came out of the barn without a black eye. I figure there's something going on if she let you get away with slinging her over your shoulder."

Feeling the blood heat his cheeks, Jake aimed for the simplest answer. "Yeah, we had a fight."

Butch nodded stiffly and walked away. Jake turned his attention back to B.J., following her and the men leading the difficult horse to an outdoor corral with a chute. But he saw Butch talking to several of the other hands. One of his men grinned and gave him the high sign, and he wondered what Butch had told them.

After B.J. had completed her examination, she walked right by Jake without saying a word. But Jake had had time to think about something that had been said earlier.

Reaching out, he again pulled her to a halt. "Aren't you going to say goodbye?"

"I thought we'd probably spoken too much to each other already today," she said, not looking at him.

"Or maybe not enough. What's this about you dining with Butch?" He knew he didn't have the right to question her movements, but he had to know.

As he expected, she stiffened beneath his hold. "I don't think that's any of your business."

He sighed. "I know. But Butch is an old friend

who just ended a messy relationship. He's vulnerable right now.'' He got her attention; that was for sure. She swung around to face him, putting her hands on her hips, which pulled apart her jean jacket. He couldn't keep from staring at her breasts beneath her plaid shirt.

''All he did was sit at our table for dinner so he wouldn't have to eat alone!'' she protested indignantly.

''Just be careful. It doesn't take much heat from you, lady, to start a forest fire.'' He reached out and traced the curve of her cheek, unable to resist touching her.

She stepped away. ''Jake, don't,'' she whispered. ''Everyone is watching.''

''I know. And that's why I'm going to give you a little kiss—just a friendly one—so everyone will know the Randalls and the Andersons are on good terms. Don't make a scene.''

That really was his intent. After all, she had expressed concern about how the county might perceive their relationship. But once his lips met hers, all caution, all planning, all good intentions went out the window. Desire, lust…good feelings replaced them, and he deepened the kiss, sweeping her into his arms.

His uninhibited crew cheered, as they had that first morning out in the pasture, and B.J. wrenched her lips from his. She didn't leave, however. Instead, she buried her face in his shirt and muttered, ''I'm going to kill you, Jake Randall. That wasn't a *friendly* kiss.''

"Well, sweetheart, it sure wasn't hostile...on either of our parts."

His sarcasm accomplished what his kiss hadn't. She jerked away from him and quickly strode to her truck parked near the barn. The dust flew as she backed up, then roared down the driveway.

Jake stood staring after her, knowing that he should've apologized instead of upsetting her even more. He almost jumped out of his skin when one of the cowboys slapped him on the back.

"Glad to see you and B.J. made up, boss. We were all pulling for you. She is one fine lady."

The man moved on without waiting for a response, but several other men grinned and waved as if agreeing with him.

"Quite a little show this morning, brother," Pete murmured as he came up beside him. "The girls are going to love hearing about this."

Jake grabbed his brother's jacket front. "You can't tell them!"

"Oh, yes, I can. When they hear about this—and you know they will—and realize I didn't tell them, Janie will have my head. Or even worse, make me sleep on the couch." Pete paused to grin. "As much as I love you, Jake, I'm not willing to make that big a sacrifice."

No, and Jake couldn't blame him. If Jake had the right to sleep with B.J., he wouldn't give it up, either.

"Besides," Pete added, distracting him, "maybe

this news will cheer up Red. His biscuits were so flat and hard this morning, I almost broke off a tooth.''

Jake watched his brother saunter away, a grin still on his face. He had a point. Red had been depressed ever since B.J. had told Mildred the truth. Red wouldn't talk about any decisions he and Mildred had come to, but it was obvious things weren't as rosy as they had been.

But B.J. wouldn't be happy that the two of them were the hot topic of gossip in the county. Even if that hadn't been his intention, he knew his behavior this morning was responsible for everyone thinking they'd had a fight and then made up.

Man, she really was going to kill him.

EVERYWHERE B.J. WENT that afternoon, she faced knowing smiles and sly innuendo about her and Jake. As best she could, she discounted any talk of the future, but frequently the best thing she could do was say nothing. Otherwise, it would be a case of protesting too much.

When she stopped by the post office to buy stamps, Mrs. Miller beamed at her.

''I hear things are looking up at the Randall spread,'' the woman said, grinning from ear to ear.

B.J. smiled and asked for two books of stamps.

''A big thaw has set in, I hear,'' the woman said, trying again.

''Really? I heard we've got a norther heading our

way, the first real big one of the season." She waited impatiently for Mrs. Miller to count out her change.

"Oh, you are a sly one, you are. But don't let Jake Randall slip through your fingers, young lady.There's too long a line waiting in case you blow it."

"Thank you for the stamps, Mrs. Miller." It was hard to return the woman's smile, but B.J. did. After all, at least things were better with this new rumor. For the past week, everywhere she went, she'd received comforting, sympathetic smiles, as if Jake had dumped her.

Her heart was not broken!

Not really. After all, she had no intention of marrying again. Her first marriage had been...nice, but her husband had been driven by the urge to make money. He hadn't been all that interested in Toby or spending quiet evenings at home. There was a fear buried deep inside her that if Darrell hadn't died so young, she would be a divorcée now rather than a widow.

She shook off her disturbing thoughts and tried to figure out what could be done about the situation she was now in, playing the role of Jake's lover. Because there was no doubt that was what the community thought. The men had given her knowing grins, and the women's remarks, about Jake and his reputed prowess with women, were downright embarrassing.

Especially when truthfully, she could only agree with them.

The moment he touched her, she melted like a Sno-Kone in the middle of a hot summer day.

It hadn't been that way with Darrell. Sex had been a part of their marriage, but B.J. hadn't hungered for his touch as she did for Jake's.

"It's probably because you haven't had sex in four years," she told herself in disgust.

Maybe she should go ahead and have an affair with him, as he'd suggested, and get him out of her system.

She almost drove off the road as she realized what she'd just thought. She must be losing her mind. An affair with Jake Randall could only bring heartache.

And what would it do to little Toby? His hopes would be raised again. And then dashed. Because Jake Randall wasn't misleading her. He didn't intend to marry again, and he'd made that fact perfectly clear.

Besides, as much as Jake valued the "right" blood inheriting his family's ranch, even if he wanted to marry her—a joke if there ever was one—she couldn't accept. She wouldn't allow Toby to be considered a second-class citizen, not in his own home.

She pulled the truck to a halt in front of her house, weary from her mental debates as much as from her work. And now she had to face the troubled looks Mildred gave her. Ever since she'd told her the truth, Mildred had refused to talk about her marriage to Red.

B.J. didn't know if she'd told Red she couldn't marry him or if she was going ahead with the marriage. Unhappily. B.J. hoped Red and Mildred would marry. But she hated herself for taking away Mildred's joy about her union.

Swinging open the door, she was stepping out of the truck when the one person she wanted to avoid appeared beside her.

"What do you want?" she snapped quickly, almost getting back in the truck again.

"I need to talk to you before you go in," Jake said. He kept a circumspect distance of several feet between them, but B.J. could feel the pull his presence always brought.

That was the major problem with Jake. It wasn't that he touched her. It was that she *wanted* him to touch her. Desperately. Now she could understand addiction. She had the same problem, only her addiction was for the touch of a sexy, hardheaded cowboy.

"What about?" she asked cautiously, determined to keep her head.

"Lucy called," he said, naming their dinner companions of last week. "She, uh, she's invited all the Randalls over for dinner tonight."

"You need me to baby-sit the twins?" That was the only connection she could make. After all, she wasn't a Randall. And wasn't likely to become one.

Jake took his hat off and ran a big hand through his hair. "Not exactly. Mildred and Red are going to be the baby-sitters."

"Fine. Toby and I can manage without Mildred.

I've been telling her that for the past week.'' She hadn't meant to sound so irritated, but she did.

"B.J., I'm sorry about this morning.''

His apology surprised her. And made her feel sad. She didn't want him to be sorry he'd tried to protect her. "It's okay. I should've explained right away.''

He grinned, and she had to fight the urge to trace his lips with her fingers. When Jake Randall smiled at her, she had trouble thinking.

"We both know there's some kind of weird chemistry going on here. Like magnets or something. We don't always act rational around each other.''

She nodded. What could she say?

"Look, B.J.—Ben and Lucy are friends. We've known Ben for forever, and Lucy almost as long.''

She nodded again. Where was this story going?

"Lucy was all happy. She's pregnant, you know.''

"I know, Jake. I was there when they told us, remember?''

He put his hat back on his head and grabbed her hands. "This is kind of hard to explain.'' His gaze didn't meet hers, and she felt her stomach turn into knots.

"What is?''

"What happened. You see, she and Ben wanted to have us all over to—to celebrate the baby, and my birthday, and all the changes going on over here. Kind of a party.''

B.J. wasn't sure she could take being this close to him much longer. In an attempt to hurry his story along, she said, "I get the picture. What's the problem?"

"One of the things she wanted to celebrate was...us."

B.J. stared at him. "Us? As in you and me?"

"Yeah."

"Jake, there is no you and me. Remember? It was a silly game that we agreed not to play anymore." Panic was filling her. She'd fought this battle, mostly with herself, once before. She didn't want to go through it again.

"Honey, I couldn't tell *her* that. And after this morning, everyone believes we had a fight and then made up. I didn't know what to say."

Drawing a deep breath, praying for control, she asked, "And what exactly did you say?"

"I said we, you and me, would be happy to come to dinner tonight with the rest of my family."

Chapter Twelve

B.J. gasped, her mind skittering in a dozen different directions as she tried to think of a response. "You didn't— Jake, that's impossible."

"No, it's not."

"Don't you get it? If we go over there as a couple, we'll be right back where we were a week ago." And she'd have to resist temptation all over again. The past week may have been dull without Jake, but at least it had been simple.

"We're already there."

"What do you mean?"

"I told you, everyone thinks we had a fight and now we've made up." His gaze didn't quite meet hers, and his cheeks were flooded with color.

"Why does everyone think that? I know you—we kissed this morning, but—"

"I was watching you, and Butch asked me if we'd had a fight and then made up." He ducked his head before finally meeting her gaze. "I told him yes, without thinking."

"But that was before you kissed me in front of everyone. Why would he ask that question?"

Jake grinned, even while he still appeared embarrassed. "'Cause the man said he figured I'd come out with a black eye unless you...cared about me."

"I—I— He's wrong!" she protested, but she knew her cheeks were even redder than Jake's. Because Butch's words were true.

"Is he? Want me to show you?" He tugged on her hands to pull her toward him.

"No! I don't need a demonstration. I was there the first time, remember?" She pulled her hands free and put them on Jake's chest to keep him apart from her.

"Yes, ma'am, you surely were," he drawled, his grin widening.

"Jake, you're getting off the subject here. What are we going to do? Stage another fight? If I go with you tonight, everyone will assume..." There was no point in saying it. Jake knew as well as she did. "I just can't go."

"Well, I'm not telling Lucy. She's been cooking all day and is excited about the party. And Mildred is the one who said you'd go."

"Mildred?" B.J. gasped, feeling betrayed. "Why would she do that? She knows we were only pretending."

"I reckon she heard the same gossip my sisters-in-law did. And they all believed it."

B.J. closed her eyes in despair. "You mean they

wanted to believe it. Didn't you tell them we were pretending?"

"Nope. It's none of their business."

Her fingers were still resting on his hard chest, growing warmer each minute. She wanted to splay her hands against his muscles, feel him pressed against him. When she realized where her thoughts were taking her, she jerked her hands away. "Jake—"

"Hi, Mr. Jake."

They both looked to the porch, to discover Toby leaning against the post, a wistful look on his face.

"Hi, sweetie, I was just coming in," B.J. said, and tried to move past Jake.

He blocked her way, his hands going to her waist. "How are you, Toby? Your mom said you were waiting until your birthday to wear your hat."

"I didn't think I should since I'm not five yet," Toby said soberly.

Jake grinned that lopsided smile that always caused her stomach to flip over, and B.J. knew her son wouldn't be able to resist it. "I think you're being a really good boy, Toby. I don't think I showed such discipline when I was your age."

Toby, as B.J. expected, returned Jake's smile. "I've been really good, Mr. Jake. I haven't had to stand in the corner or anything."

"Good for you, son. Will you be ready for the Halloween party on Friday? Got your monster costume ready?"

Before Toby could answer, B.J. whispered, "Jake, let me by."

She was a little surprised when he readily stepped aside, but he immediately looped an arm around her shoulders and walked with her to the porch.

"Yeah. I'm gonna be *real* scary!"

"All right! And you're going to stay with Red and Mildred again tonight?"

Jake ignored B.J.'s attempts to shrug off his arm, but she saw Toby staring at them. She'd explained so carefully that she and Jake wouldn't be kissing again. How would Toby interpret Jake's behavior?

"Mommy said she wasn't going to go places with you anymore," Toby said slowly, continuing to stare at them.

Jake looked down at her, one eyebrow sliding up before he turned his attention back to her son. "Well, Toby, it's like this. Your mom was unhappy with me. But ladies change their minds all the time. I told her I was sorry."

"Oh. Like when I've been bad and I say I'm sorry?"

Jake nodded, still smiling.

Toby really grinned. "Oh, good. 'Cause Mommy always kisses me and forgives me."

"Exactly." He came to a stop, pulling B.J. around to face him. Leaning closer, he whispered, "We'll figure out what to do later. But you'll have to come tonight if you're not going to upset Lucy." Then he brushed his lips across hers, lightly this time. "I'll be back in an hour."

He waved to Toby and strode across the yard, leaving B.J. standing like a statue, her mind seething with ways to punish the man. He was driving her crazy!

AFTER DINNER that evening at the Turnbulls', B.J. followed the rest of the women into the kitchen. Though Lucy protested she didn't need any help, they ignored her.

B.J. wasn't reluctant to help, but she was hesitant to be alone with her friends. She'd felt all of them watching her and Jake all evening. If he so much as touched her hand, everyone's eyes had been trained on them.

To be alone with the women now meant she would have to answer questions. And she had no answers. None at all.

She'd tried to come up with a reason for refusing to attend, but Jake was right. She couldn't refuse without appearing terribly rude. And she couldn't be angry with Mildred. After all, she had been told about the morning's events. It was B.J.'s fault, hers and Jake's, that everyone thought they were dating again.

That stupid kiss.

The one in front of everyone.

She'd told Mildred again this evening, before she left, that the kiss was a mistake, that she and Jake weren't—whatever. Mildred had apologized for accepting the invitation for her, but there had been a look in her aunt's eyes that told B.J. she hadn't convinced her.

"What a lovely dinner, Lucy," Megan said as she carried dirty dishes to the sink. "I'd love the recipe for that casserole. Did you see the way Chad ate it? I don't dare tell Red."

"I'd be glad to give you a copy of it. It's one of my mother's." Lucy began organizing the dishes and rinsing them.

"This has been so much fun," Janie said.

"We don't socialize enough," Lucy agreed. "But we have the party at your house in two days. Are you all ready?"

"Almost," Janie said. "Of course, we have Red and Mildred to handle a lot of the work." She looked at B.J. out of the corner of her eye. "Mildred is a godsend."

"Yes, she's wonderful, isn't she?" B.J. agreed, hoping the conversation would stay on the party.

"Yeah. Will you miss her when she and Red marry?" Anna asked.

Uh-oh. B.J. got nervous whenever the subject turned to marriage. "Of course we'll miss her, but we'll manage. We want Mildred to be happy."

"It's so nice, the way things have worked out," Anna said with a happy sigh. "No one's alone while the rest of us are happy."

Stark silence followed her words. B.J. was careful not to look at anyone.

Finally Megan said, "Anna didn't mean to leap to

conclusions, B.J., but you know we're all hopeful that you and Jake—"

"Jake and I are friends, that's all. It's awkward around here not to be a couple." B.J. hoped they believed her.

"Then you're not—" Lucy began, and then halted, blushing. "I mean, the other night we got the impression that the two of you— That is, you seem to make such a nice couple."

"No! No, we're not a couple. There's nothing between us. In fact, I would describe our relationship as a, uh, professional one. I work as Jake's vet, and that's all."

B.J. was standing with her back to the door to the dining room and didn't realize anyone was entering until strong arms wrapped around her and Jake kissed her cheek.

"Hi, honey. You got dishpan hands yet?"

Closing her eyes, B.J. fought to hold back a groan. Had he heard her words? Or was he still role-playing? She'd noticed during the dinner he had treated her much as his brothers treated their wives, but he hadn't caressed her in any way. There had been a gentle playfulness, but no actual flirtation. Until now. How could she explain this?

"Jake!" she protested even as the others chuckled.

"What?" he asked, turning her around to face him.

"I just explained to the others that we're not—not a couple! Now what are they going to think?" Better to face him than the knowing smiles on her friends' faces.

"Probably that I can't keep my hands off you. That's what the guys are saying." He grinned as if he were happy about their conclusion.

"Stop acting!" She spun around to the women. "Really, Jake's just teasing. We're not a couple."

Instead of backing her up, Jake drawled, "Well, honey, we're a couple in the sense that there's two of us. But we're not a couple who's going to get married. We've both tried marriage, and I, for one, can do without that complication in my life."

B.J. should've been pleased as she watched the happiness fade from her friends' expressions. After all, Jake had done a good job of explaining their situation. But her heart felt heavy. Probably because Jake had kind of left it hanging that they might have a relationship, just not a legal one.

"Sometimes it's awkward to be alone when everyone else is a couple. Jake and I are helping each other out," she added, stepping away from him before her body gave her away.

She sat down at the kitchen table and looked at Jake. His eyes narrowed, as if in challenge to her words. She couldn't imagine what he had to complain about. She'd only echoed his sentiments.

"But, Jake, surely you don't compare B.J. to Chloe? Can't you see that B.J. is our kind? That she'd make a wonderful wife?" Janie insisted.

"Janie!" B.J. protested.

"Janie," Jake joined her in saying, but he continued, "I told the boys to warn you about matchmaking. I'm happy the way I am. There are enough happy couples and babies at our house. Leave well enough alone." By the time he finished, his voice was stern.

Turning to Lucy, he said, "I apologize for letting family things intrude, Lucy. You fixed a wonderful meal, and we all enjoyed ourselves. I came in here to ask if you ladies weren't going to join us. We're lonesome."

His dramatic complaint raised laughter that eased an awkward moment, and there was a general movement toward the door.

"We've finished," Lucy said. "We wouldn't want you men to be lonesome."

B.J. moved faster than the others. Right now she didn't care if Jake was lonesome or not. In fact, she would like him to be lonesome! But she also didn't want to be alone with him.

An hour later, she couldn't avoid him, since he'd driven the two of them to Ben and Lucy's. She'd tried to catch a ride with one of his brothers, but Jake made sure she didn't succeed.

Once they were alone in the truck, he turned to her. "What are you trying to do? Embarrass me in front of my brothers?" he demanded, anger in his voice.

"Why not? You embarrassed me in front of my friends." She refused to look at him.

"What are you talking about? I didn't do any such

thing." He gunned the engine and roared down the driveway to the road.

"You *implied* that we were going to have an affair, or were already. I don't appreciate my reputation being smeared."

"Maybe your reputation wouldn't be smeared. Maybe it would be boosted if everyone thought you were having an affair with me."

There was a challenge in his voice, but B.J. wasn't intimidated. "How arrogant! Do you think you're that wonderful?"

"Nope. But I think you've gotten a reputation for being a cold fish."

She was stunned by his words. "What are you talking about?"

"A lot of the guys have asked you out, flirted with you, but you haven't responded."

"How can you—?" She turned bright red as she thought about her response to this man.

"Hey, I'm not complaining, lady. If you responded any more to my kisses, we would know each other a lot better than we do. But you'll have to admit you don't usually let anyone get that close."

Now her cheeks were flame red, and she stared straight ahead of her into the darkness. "I didn't think it would be a good idea to mix business with—with pleasure. I don't like to date my customers."

"I think maybe you're just afraid to get close to anyone. I'm wondering if maybe your marriage

wasn't as good as you'd like people to believe."
His voice cut through the shadows, making her
angrier.

She wasn't interested in discussing her marriage
with Jake Randall. It was none of his business. Going
on the attack, she said, "I don't think you have any
room to talk, Jake. Your marriage wasn't a blue-
ribbon winner."

"Nope. But I never pretended it was. That's why
I don't intend to marry again."

"I think you've made that abundantly clear.
And I'd appreciate it if you'd keep your distance.
That flirting routine you pulled in the kitchen has to
stop!"

"Hey, I thought you wanted people to think we
were dating. I was only playing the game."

"The game is over. I told you!"

He turned off the road onto Randall property without responding to her curt words. She didn't care. Too
many times she'd let him touch her, even encouraged
him, but now the touching had to stop.

Everything had to stop. No more pretense.

No more Jake.

"Just like that?"

"Yes, just like that. If anyone has the audacity to
ask what happened, just tell them you dumped me."
She didn't care if people thought Jake didn't want her.
It was the truth. He didn't want her forever, and that
was the only way she could consider— She shook her
head to dismiss such silly hopes.

"I'm not sure they'll believe me, since I haven't been able to keep my hands off of you," he growled.

"They will if you'll keep your distance."

"Hey, I'm not the only one who needs this lecture. You didn't exactly fight me off, honey. Maybe I wouldn't keep coming back if you ever said no." He pulled his truck to a stop. His brothers and their wives were right behind them in the sedan. When B.J. reached for the door handle, she discovered Jake's hand over hers. "Wait," he said in a low voice.

"Why?"

"Because I don't think we've finished this discussion."

"Yes, we have, Jake. There's nothing more to discuss, nothing more to do. I'll keep my distance. You keep your insinuations to yourself. It's over."

"Fine!" he snapped, releasing her hand. "And next time don't involve me in your schemes!"

Her mouth worked as she tried to find the words to lambast him. Finally she sputtered, "You started it!"

"You continued it!" he returned.

In the light from the porch, she could see his eyes snap with anger. She pretended she didn't care. After all, she was fighting for survival, hopefully with her heart intact. "So we'll *both* finish it. Good night, Jake!"

This time he didn't stop her from opening the truck door. She slid out and ran the short distance to her house and safety.

As SOON AS the Randall men left the house the next morning, Mildred and Red joined the female side of the family at the breakfast table.

"How did it go last night?" Red asked.

Anna sighed. "It was a nice evening, but…"

"Yes?" Mildred prodded, leaning forward eagerly.

"Jake admitted he's attracted to B.J., couldn't keep his hands off her, in fact, but—"

"Good!" Red interjected.

"Nope," Janie said. "It's not good. He announced, in front of B.J., that he had no intention of marrying. But he wasn't averse to anything else she would agree to."

Mildred gasped. "B.J. is a nice girl!"

Red squared his jaw, clearly intent on defending his own. "B.J. is a woman, Millie, not a girl, and Jake wouldn't do anything she didn't agree to."

"Whatever they do, that's not the point," Janie quickly said before an argument could break out. "We want them *married.* We want Jake to have kids, too. We want Toby to have a daddy. We want—"

"But it has to be what *they* want, too," Megan said.

"I think it's what they both want, but they're afraid," Anna said softly. "Jake's always touching her and watching her. And B.J. blushes every time he gets near."

"That's sex, not love," Red said.

"Well, then, you and Mildred must not love each other," Janie argued, "because those words describe the two of you." She stared at his arm on the back of Mildred's chair, his hand touching her shoulder.

Red jerked his hand away, and Mildred blushed.

"We're different! We care about each other. We're not just out for what we can get," Red assured them.

"Isn't that what Jake was doing yesterday morning when he didn't want B.J. working on Pete's horse? Caring for her?" Anna asked.

"That's right," Mildred seconded. "He was trying to protect her. And he spends a lot of time with Toby."

"So how do we convince bullheaded Jake that he needs to get married?" Janie asked.

Silence fell as they each contemplated the question.

Finally Anna said, "We've invited all the single women we know to pursue Jake, so he'll turn to B.J."

Janie shook her head. "I know, but— Of course! Why didn't I think of it before?"

"What?" Megan demanded. "Don't keep us in suspense."

"We need to invite all the single *men!*"

Red frowned, staring at Janie. "But won't they just flirt with all the single women? Cancel each other out?"

"Some of them, yes. But B.J. is a beautiful woman. With the right encouragement from interested parties—" she winked at the rest of them "—some of the men will pursue her. I think Jake might not like sharing B.J."

Recognition dawned on all their faces.

"Good plan, Janie," Red agreed. "Jealousy always works."

"At least it can't hurt," Mildred agreed. "And if Jake isn't interested, maybe B.J. will find someone else to plan a future with."

Loud protests rose from the rest of the conspirators.

"We've already claimed B.J. as a Randall," Janie said, speaking for everyone. "And we'll convince Jake of that fact, come hell or high water." She raised her coffee cup. "Here's to Operation Halloween. May Cupid plant an arrow in Jake's heart."

"Here, here!" the others agreed in unison, raising their cups.

Red had the last word, however. "I just hope Cupid can recognize him under his mask."

Chapter Thirteen

Jake was appalled.

"You're kidding me, Anna!" When she continued to stare at him innocently, her blue eyes wide, he added weakly, "Aren't you?"

"No, Jake," Anna replied. "I picked it out especially for you. You'll look great in it."

"Anna," he began in frustration, staring at the costume waiting on his bed, "it's a dress!"

"No, Jake, it's a toga. You're going to be Mark Antony." When he didn't show any appreciation for her explanation, she added, "And you get to carry a spear."

"Anna, I'll be the only man there in a skirt." Jake had a terrible time denying Anna anything, but he'd be damned if he'd strut around in a skirt in front of his neighbors.

"No, you won't. Brett is going as a Scot. We're wearing matching kilts."

She beamed at him, and Jake felt his resistance

slipping. Desperately he said, "I'm the host. I don't think I should wear a costume."

"Jake, you have to!" she pleaded. "We told everyone they had to wear a costume. Your brothers will be furious if you didn't have one. Besides, I picked this one out special for you."

He gave up. He should've known from the beginning that she would win. "Okay, okay. But the first guy who laughs at me goes home with a broken nose."

"Thank you, Jake," Anna said, and reached up to kiss his cheek. Then she slipped from his bedroom, leaving Jake wondering how he'd gotten himself into this situation.

His sisters-in-law had announced last week that they were going to Casper to find costumes for everyone, but he hadn't paid much attention to their plans. He hadn't been in the mood to care. Besides, he figured he'd be a ghost, or maybe a pirate.

He stared at the sandals that were supposed to crisscross up his leg to his knee. Sandals in October in Wyoming? His toes might freeze off tonight.

Eyeing the toga, which would stop just above his knees, he realized he might be concerned about more than his toes freezing off.

"LAND'S SAKE, CHILD," Mildred fussed, pushing B.J. down the hall, "of all nights to be late. We're supposed to be at the party right now. Toby and I are dressed already."

B.J. didn't need her aunt to tell her. Mildred didn't normally dress as a Gypsy dancer. "What's Red wearing?"

Mildred grinned, but her cheeks were pink. "He's a Gypsy, too."

"Ah. Well, you and Toby can go on over as soon as I've seen his costume. I'll find something to wear and be over in a few minutes." She was tired. A quick appearance at the party would satisfy courtesy and then, when it was Toby's bedtime, the two of them would slip away. B.J. had no intention of spending any more time at the Randall house than she had to.

"Oh, you don't have to worry. You already have a costume. You're going as Cleopatra."

B.J. frowned. She hadn't given much thought to her costume, but she'd certainly never considered the Egyptian queen. "Why Cleopatra?"

"The girls found it in Casper. It's perfect for you with your hair unbraided and the snake thing across your forehead."

B.J. just stopped herself from asking why a snake thing was perfect for her. With a sigh, she agreed, "Okay, but I have to shower first."

"I know. Just hurry."

Twenty minutes later, B.J. stared at herself in the mirror. The one-shouldered white dress, with a gold belt in a snake motif that matched her headband, flowed flatteringly to the floor with a discreet slit on one side to midthigh.

But she felt overexposed with her bare shoulder.

"You look beautiful," Mildred said, a reverent tone in her voice.

"Don't be silly, Mildred. I think I look ridiculous."

Mildred laughed. "We'll see. Put on that bracelet and those gold sandals while I turn off the video Toby's watching. Do you have the gifts ready?"

"Yes," B.J. said, but she bit her lip as Mildred turned away. She had debated long and hard over what to get Jake. He was a man who had just about everything he wanted.

Only a chance remark by Megan about Jake's fascination with the Western writer Zane Grey solved her problem. Instead of buying Jake something he didn't need, she'd wrapped up a copy of *Riders of the Purple Sage,* autographed by the author himself. Her father had long cherished the book, and it had come to B.J. upon his death. She knew her father would be happy to have his treasure go to someone who would appreciate it.

Now, however, she had no intention of giving Jake Randall a gift. Especially one he might think was too personal. One that might make him think she cared about him.

She started to leave the bedroom without the present for Jake when her son met her at the door.

"Where's Mr. Jake's present? I want to carry it."

"Um, I don't think we should take it to him tonight, sweetie. We'll give him a present another time." She'd buy him a box of candy or some other impersonal gift.

"No, Mommy, we have to give it to him tonight. Please?"

B.J. stared down at her son. How could she disappoint him? How could she teach him about generosity, kindness, thoughtfulness by her petty behavior?

With a sigh, she turned back into her bedroom and picked up one of the wrapped presents, one for Jake and one for Toby. "Okay, Toby, here is Mr. Jake's gift."

For Toby, who'd already opened several presents, she'd bought indestructible plastic trucks. She figured all the children present could play with them without their being destroyed.

"Come on!" Mildred called. "We're late."

"Coming," B.J. returned. With reluctance, she picked up the other gift and started toward the door. At the last minute, she remembered the cold air that had escorted her home. A front was supposed to move in tonight.

"Mildred? You'd better grab a coat. It's getting cold outside."

"A coat? Is the weather changing?"

"Yes. I wouldn't be surprised to see snow by the time we start home." At least, by the time Mildred started home. B.J. and Toby would already be snug in their beds.

"Mommy," Toby called from behind her, "I forgot to scare you!"

He looked quite different in his Batman costume,

but she knelt to give him a hug anyway. "Oh, my, yes, I'm scared. You'd better hug me so I won't be."

"I'm not supposed to hug you. Mr. Jake is. I'm the one who's *scaring* you, Mommy," Toby complained even as he threw his arms around her neck.

"I know, but thanks for the hug anyway. Ready to go? Get your coat."

"But it'll cover up my costume."

"As soon as we get in the door, you can take it off."

"Okay." When he appeared only seconds later, he not only had on his coat, but also atop his Batman ears sat his dark gray cowboy hat.

"I'm wearing my new hat. Mr. Jake will like that, won't he?"

B.J. couldn't deny her son's words. She knew Jake wanted Toby to like his new hat. She just didn't think it would be a good idea for Toby to concern himself much with Jake. "Yes, sweetie."

Mildred opened the door. "Ooh. You're right about that norther, B.J. It's much colder out there. Come on. We'll want to walk fast."

"Aunt Mildred, how come you make noise when you walk?" Toby asked as he followed her to the door.

"It's these beads. They rattle against each other. Good thing I'm not planning on sneaking up on anyone. Oh, I almost forgot! Here's your mask, B.J."

"Mask? Isn't the costume enough?"

"Nope. You have to wear this gold mask, too. At

least for a while. I bet a lot of people won't guess it's you. They've never seen you with your hair down.''

"Yeah. Your hair is pretty, Mommy.''

"Thanks, Toby. But I think everyone will know who I am.''

"What will Mr. Jake be wearing? Will he come dressed as a cowboy?''

"Probably,'' B.J. said, finding it difficult to imagine Jake as anything but himself.

Which made the first thing she saw when she entered the living room at the Randalls hard to believe.

JAKE HAD WON a promise from Anna that he could change into jeans once the party was under way. Because one look at his bare knees was enough to make him want to hide in the bathroom and never come down at all.

In the meantime, however, he'd had to don the fake laurel wreath, strap up the sandals and greet his neighbors in the short toga. He'd received some wolf whistles from the men, grinning from ear to ear and, even more embarrassing, some ogling from the ladies.

"Hey, Jake, I hear they need some more contestants in the Miss Wyoming contest,'' Ben called from a short distance away. He knew better than to get close.

"I'm paying you back, Ben. I'm paying all of you back for your words this evening. You won't know when to expect it, but you can be sure it's coming.'' He added a smile to his warning, but it was fiendish rather than friendly. Some of the women clapped at his words, and he swept a bow, keeping his back to the fireplace. He didn't want to bend over in front of anyone. He'd embarrass himself.

As he rose, he stared at the most beautiful creature he'd ever seen, standing in the doorway of the living room. Cleopatra, a gold snake coiled about her head, black hair spilling in a glorious cloud almost to her waist, her tall, willowy form clad in a flowing white robe caught around her small waist with a gold belt, stared back at him. Her face was covered with a gold half mask.

"Mark Antony, it's your Cleopatra!" Chad called out.

Jake hadn't made the connection between their costumes. Nor had he consciously identified the woman. Until now.

But everyone else in the room had.

He crossed the room and took her hand, raising it to his lips. Then he lifted his gaze, leaned over and murmured, "I'm going to wring Anna's neck. Sorry, I didn't plan this."

"I didn't think you had. As usual, our families are one step ahead of us," Cleopatra, aka B.J., murmured. "All we can do is smile and put the best face on it."

"That's easy for you to say. At least your costume shows off your beauty."

She gave him a cool stare. "Your costume shows off…a lot of you."

"Don't you start, too, B.J. It's been downright embarrassing, the way the women have been looking at me. I feel like a slab of beef at a barbecue."

One slim brow arched up toward the gold band on her forehead. "Now you know how women feel."

He was tempted to slide his arms around her and pull her against him, but he could tell she was still angry with him. So he settled for leaning near her and saying, "Yeah, I've felt a few, but none of them have felt as good as you."

Her full lips tightened, drawing his attention, and she started to move away.

"You're still mad at me, aren't you?" he asked under his breath, aware that everyone was watching them. For the past several days, he'd done nothing but think about the dissolution of their...whatever it had been. Their pretense. He'd missed it. He'd missed seeing B.J. He'd missed touching her.

"No, not at all," she said calmly, nodding and smiling at their guests over his shoulder. "Excuse me?"

He caught her arm as she tried to move away. "There's no need to act as if we've never even spoken to each other," he protested. "We're friends, aren't we?"

Her gaze returned to his face, and he almost shivered from the coldness it showed. "No, Jake, I don't think we're friends. We used each other, but it's over. That's all."

This time, when she tried to move away, he let her go. As she strolled across the room, he got a glimpse of long leg through the slit. "Is that dress legal?" he muttered, thinking aloud.

Butch must've just walked up beside him, because he cleared his throat. "I don't think so. It's enough to make you salivate, isn't it?"

When Jake glared at him, he held up a hand. "Just thinking out loud."

Just as Jake relaxed, turning his gaze back to Cleopatra, Butch spoke again. "But I'm a little confused."

"What do you mean?"

"Janie told me there was nothing between you and B.J. She suggested I cozy on up to the lady, ask her out."

"Janie did what?" Jake whipped back, his eyes blazing. He couldn't believe what his friend was telling him. He'd begun to suspect that his sisters-in-law had been setting red herrings with those other women, intending him for B.J. all along.

That had been one reason for him announcing at Ben and Lucy's what his intentions toward B.J. were. He didn't want any misunderstandings.

Which didn't explain why he was upset now.

"You heard me. So, tell me, boss, is she yours or isn't she?" Butch waited, his gaze clear, for Jake to stake his claim on B.J....or back off.

Damn. Jake knew he couldn't honestly claim B.J. as his own. That would involve commitment, and he wanted none of that. Commitment meant you put your heart on the line, and risked it getting trampled.

But he sure as hell didn't want every man in the county thinking B.J. was fair game. In spite of what she'd just said, he knew they had unfinished business to work out. But he couldn't lie to Butch.

He finally muttered, "B.J.'s a free woman."

"May the best man win?" Butch probed.

"Yeah." He didn't have to wait long for Butch's reaction. The cowboy made a beeline for B.J.

And Jake decided to have a little chat with Janie Randall.

He didn't see her in the living room, so he headed for the kitchen. Red was preparing another plate to take to the dining room for the buffet.

"You seen Janie?"

"Nope. Not in the last few minutes. I bet she's upstairs getting the boys ready. She said something about dressing them up for Halloween."

Jake wandered back to the living room. His gaze immediately flew to B.J., holding court much as Cleopatra might have done, surrounded by handsome men.

Staring, Jake realized just about every single man in the county was there, some of them even sitting on the floor, at her feet. She had removed the gold mask and, as he watched, she threw her head back and laughed at something one of the men had said. Jake ground his teeth.

Unable to stop himself, he crossed to the group. "B.J., Mildred needs to see you in the kitchen."

As he'd known she would, she rose at once. "Of course. Excuse me, gentlemen."

He followed her from the room, down the hall, admiring the way the silky costume clung to her, enjoying the occasional glimpse of leg as she walked. Red was coming out as they entered.

"Oops. Excuse me," he said, juggling two plates. "I'll be right back."

B.J. smiled at him and then pushed the door open. "Why are you following me?" she asked Juke as they entered the kitchen. Then, a frown on her face, she turned back around. "Mildred isn't here."

"I know."

Staring at him intently, she said, "She never asked me to come here, did she?"

"Nope."

"What's going on, Jake?"

"I'm not sure, but I think we're being manipulated again." He watched her carefully and was relieved to see she had no idea what he was talking about.

"Explain yourself." She crossed her arms under her breasts and looked every bit the autocratic but always sexy Cleopatra.

"Butch told me Janie encouraged him to ask you out."

He couldn't tell what she was thinking, though there was a tinge of surprise on her face briefly.

"And?"

"Well? Isn't that enough? Suddenly you're surrounded by every eligible bachelor within a hundred miles, and you don't put two and two together?"

"Are you saying those men are only paying any attention to me because your sisters-in-law encouraged them? Or maybe even bribed them? That I'm so unattractive no man would come within a mile of me unless one of the great Randalls told them to? Thank you very much, Jake. You've just made my night!"

She immediately turned to take flight, but he caught her arm. "Don't be ridiculous!" He couldn't conceive that she could possibly believe what she'd just said. Didn't the woman know she made him go weak in the knees, just looking at her?

"Turn loose of me!"

"B.J., you're the most beautiful woman here tonight and you know it! Even the married men can't keep their eyes off you and that blasted costume. Do you realize how high that slit is?"

Though her cheeks turned a little red, she looked him up and down and said, "About as high as *your* skirt."

"Aw, now that's hittin' below the belt, Barbara Jo," he said, grinning.

"No one but Mildred ever calls me that." She raised her chin in challenge.

He moved a little closer and tried to put a smile on her face. "I was trying to distract you from my knobbly knees."

"You're being ridiculous, Jake." She tried to push past him, but he blocked her way. "I need to get back to the living room before people start remembering that we left together. They'll think the worst.''

''Which is?'' he probed.

Her cheeks flushed, and she took a step backward. ''That we're having a romantic interlude somewhere.''

He almost salivated at the thought. Why did this one woman stir his senses? Why did this one woman drive him crazy? Why did the thought of other men— Jake stood, turned to stone. The answer was more than he could understand, accept. Because it meant he'd gone back on the promise he'd made to himself when Chloe had left.

He'd sworn he'd never love another woman. He'd never put his happiness in another's hands. And most certain of all, he'd never marry again.

It was too late. That was the most amazing part. He'd already broken those first two promises. And he wanted to break the other as soon as possible.

He wanted to marry B. J. Anderson.

''Are you going to let me by?'' she asked, her voice tense.

Panic filled him, mixed with desire, and he had no answer for her. All he could do was stare at her.

The sound of the door opening behind him stopped him from answering B.J. He turned to face Janie, with Pete right behind.

''Uh, are we interrupting something?'' Pete asked.

''No,'' B.J. quickly replied. ''I was just leaving.''

''Don't go on our account,'' Janie quickly said.

"And if you're wanting to be alone, we can tell you a few good places." She grinned at both of them, as if they were all coconspirators.

Jake sneaked a look at B.J. Her cheeks were flaming, and she wouldn't look at him, even though he willed her to.

"No, thank you. I was looking for Mildred. I think it's about time for me and Toby to go home," B.J. muttered, not looking at anyone.

"Wait, B.J. I think we need to have a little discussion with Janie before you go." Anything to keep her there, near him.

"What about?" Janie asked.

"I think you, and probably the other two female Randalls, have been interfering again," Jake said, trying to keep his voice stern.

"Interfering in what?" Janie asked, not looking the least bit guilty, as Jake expected her to.

"Yeah, Jake," Pete seconded. "Interfering in what?"

Well, now, there was the problem. Exactly what should Jake call this situation. His romance with B.J.? It wasn't really a romance. At least, he'd suddenly realized it was on his part, but he hadn't broken the news to B.J.

"Uh, mine and B.J.'s lives."

Anna raised her eyebrows. "Just how am I interfering with your lives?"

"You encouraged Butch to ask B.J. out." His

voice was surer now. After all, he was quite clear about that fact.

"All I did was *suggest* Butch ask B.J. out."

B.J., who'd been edging toward the door, smiled at Janie. "Thanks, Janie. He did. We're going to dinner next weekend." Then she walked out the door.

Jake stared after her, his heart contracting. Had he blown his relationship with B.J.? Had he realized too late that life without her was not worth living?

Chapter Fourteen

Ranch people weren't prone to staying up late. By ten o'clock everyone was saying his or her goodbyes. Their leaving was hastened by the storm that blew in. The first snow of the season was dusting the landscape with whiteness.

Jake, still in his toga in spite of his plans, waved the last of their guests goodbye, except for Mildred, B.J. and Toby. He had made Janie promise to keep the Andersons there until he unwrapped his gifts.

He'd been helped by Toby, even if the boy didn't realize the favor he'd done him. B.J. had tried to leave early, but Toby had pleaded to stay until Jake opened his presents.

He knew B.J. wouldn't have stayed willingly. After that little scene in the kitchen, she'd avoided him. And flirted with the men crowding around her.

With gritted teeth, he'd tried to ignore her. As he'd visited with his friends and neighbors, however, he hadn't been able to keep his gaze from straying to her. And he'd provided an entertaining evening for his audience.

They hadn't hesitated to let him know about it, either. Ben had clapped him on the shoulder and warned him he'd better stake his claim before she escaped. Mr. Miller asked him when he'd be shopping for a ring. The pastor had hinted about another Randall wedding.

Only one thing had kept him from losing his mind. B.J. couldn't keep from watching him, too.

Ceci and some of the other ladies had pursued him, teasing him about his costume. Every time one of them got close to him, he'd catch B.J. watching.

Now, as he entered the living room, she stood. "We really should be going."

"Jake has to open his birthday presents," Megan said. "You have to stay for that."

"It should just be family. We're—"

"Going to be family. After all, Red and Mildred are engaged," Pete said. "And it's not as if you have to drive a long way in the snow."

B.J. didn't speak, only shrugging her shoulders. Since one of them was bare, that movement heightened Jake's blood pressure considerably. He wanted to touch her bare skin, to slide his hand—

"Well, Jake, aren't you eager to open your presents?" Anna asked.

He stopped staring at B.J. and smiled. "Sure. Where are they?"

He soon had several small boxes in front of him.

Inside one of them was a pair of good leather work gloves from Red and Mildred. "I've been needing a new pair, but these are almost too nice to mess up. Thanks." He smiled at the couple, sitting together, their hands entwined.

The next box was extremely light. When he opened it, he discovered it was empty. Raising one eyebrow, he said, "Are you trying to tell me something?"

"Nope, but the real present was too big to wrap," Pete assured him, and left the room. He returned only seconds later with a saddle slung over his shoulder. The leather was elaborately cut with flourishes, and the name Randall was carved into the back of the seat. Toby, half-asleep next to his mother, came awake and knelt on the floor beside Jake, running his fingers over the polished leather.

"Wow, Mr. Jake, it's beautiful!"

"Yeah, it is," Jake agreed. He looked at his brothers and their wives, fighting to hide the emotion that filled him. "Toby's right. Thank you. I've never seen anything so beautiful."

Toby, still rubbing the leather, said, "Someday I'm going to have me a saddle, too. And a horse. I'm going to be a cowboy, too." He beamed up at Jake, hero worship on his face, and Jake felt his heart turn over.

He didn't care much for what he'd heard about B.J.'s husband, but he couldn't help but feel sorry for the man. He'd fathered a terrific boy, and he didn't get to be around to see him grow up.

He pulled the little boy to him and hugged him. "Those are great plans, Toby. Maybe tomorrow we'll try out my new saddle together."

"Really, Mr. Jake?" Toby asked, slinging one arm around Jake's neck and leaning against him.

"Really," Jake agreed, grinning. Until his gaze collided with B.J.'s.

She was staring at him, her hazel eyes dark with some emotion he couldn't read. But he didn't think it was approval, because those full lips that fascinated him were turned down on the edges.

"There's another present," Anna urged.

Jake picked up the last box.

"It's from me and Mommy!" Toby informed him, bouncing on his toes beside him. "I told Mommy we should buy you something, but she said you'd want this."

"Toby," B.J. said softly, "I think you need to give Mr. Jake some room. Come back over here."

"He's all right, B.J.," Jake said, keeping Toby beside him, his arm around him.

He watched Toby look at his mother for her approval. She gave a brief nod and a smile for her child, but when she looked at Jake, the smile disappeared.

Removing the paper carefully, he lifted the lid on the box and discovered the old book. Carefully he took the Zane Grey book from the box and opened it. A first edition. He looked up to tell her how wonderful her gift was, but Toby, turning the pages, spoke first.

"Mommy! Somebody wrote in the book. We have to get Mr. Jake another present. This one is messed up."

Jake looked at the page where Toby was pointing. The author's signature jumped up at him. He slowly raised his gaze to B.J., hoping she could see how much the gift meant to him.

"No, Toby, this is the perfect gift. That's the signature of the man who wrote the book." There were several gasps from those gathered around, but he ignored them all, concentrating on B.J. "Thank you. This is a magnificent gift."

She shrugged those shoulders again, and he thought he was going to explode. In spite of his enjoyment of his family, gathered around, sharing the moment with him, he wished he and B.J. were alone. He wanted to thank her again and again.

And he wanted to hold her. To feel her heat against him, to stroke that bare shoulder, to feel her lips move beneath his.

Chad moved to look over his shoulder at the signature. "Wow, I'm impressed. An autographed first edition. Where did you find it, B.J.?"

She suddenly seemed embarrassed. "It—it was my father's. Come on, Toby. Time to get you to bed." She rose, had Toby by the hand and was halfway out of the room before anyone else could move.

"Wait!" Jake ordered, putting his precious gift aside and rising.

She stopped and looked at him, but he could tell

he wouldn't hold her long. Desperately he turned to Mildred. "Could you take Toby home? I need to speak with B.J. for a few minutes."

Red stood and pulled Mildred up from the couch. "We'll both take the little guy home and tuck him in. Okay with you, Toby?"

"No, that's not necessary. I can—" B.J. began, but Mildred cut her off.

"The least you can do is talk to Jake, B.J. He's been a good host tonight. And he's celebrating his birthday. Toby will be fine with us." Without waiting for B.J. to agree, she and Red crossed the room and took Toby's hand. "Tell everyone good-night, Toby."

He did as Mildred said, but when he got to Jake, he turned loose of Mildred's hand and ran back to Jake to hug him around his neck. "Happy birthday, Mr. Jake."

Jake loved the feel of Toby's arms around his neck. He hugged the boy back. "Happy birthday to you, Toby. I'll see you tomorrow, and we'll try out that saddle."

Toby gave him his megawatt smile that warmed his heart and ran back to Red and Mildred. After the threesome walked out of the room, his brothers and their wives hastily began making excuses to absent themselves.

"It's all right. B.J. and I will go to the barn. We need a little privacy," Jake said in response.

"It'll be cold out there. There's plenty of room in this house," Pete assured him.

"It's not that cold out yet. Come on, B.J." He didn't want her worrying about someone walking in on them. And he didn't want to worry about it, either.

He wasn't clear about the need to see her alone. He didn't have any great plans. But he wanted to thank her for the incredible gift she'd given him. And he wanted to tell her she shouldn't flirt with those other men.

And he wanted to touch her.

"No, Jake, we should talk here," she insisted.

He ignored her, crossing the room and clasping her hand in his.

He led her to the kitchen, where he handed her her coat and grabbed one for himself. Then he took her hand again and led her to the door. Once they got outside, they didn't waste any time. The cold wind pushed them along.

"Man, I don't know how women wear skirts in winter," Jake complained as he closed the barn door behind them and switched on the light.

"Your legs get cold?" she asked, her voice husky.

"A lot more than my legs." He grinned at her, but then his grin faded as they stared at each other.

She abruptly moved away, wrapping her arms around her. "Why are we here, Jake? What do you have to say?"

"A lot. So we might as well get comfortable." He strode to the tack room at the back of the barn.

"It's late, Jake. I can't stay long," she called out, but he ignored her.

Several blankets were kept in the storage room for late nights if one of them had to stay up with a mare giving birth or a horse that was sick. He spread one out on a pile of hay and kept the other to cover with.

"Come on, B.J., sit down."

She shook her head no. "That would be like Hansel and Gretel bending over to peek in the oven. The wicked witch shoved them in."

"There's no wicked witch here, B.J. But I want to thank you for that incredible gift. And I'd like to keep my legs warm while I'm doing it. They're going to turn blue any moment."

"You're the one who wanted to come out here. And my dress isn't exactly suited to this weather, either."

"I know. It was a pleasure to watch you walk around tonight." He smiled but he hoped she couldn't read his mind. If she could, she'd be out of that barn faster than a charging bull.

"Jake Randall! You can't seem to keep your mind off— Never mind. You're welcome for the gift. I have to go now."

"I have something else to tell you," he said quickly. He breathed a sigh of relief when she turned around to face him again.

"What?"

"Come on over here and sit down. I'm not going to bite you."

She hesitated and then slowly walked toward him. He drank in the sight of her graceful movement, her silky hair, those long legs. When she sank down on the blanket, keeping several feet between them, he shook out the second blanket and let it fall over the two of them.

"What did you have to say?"

"Does your hair help keep you warm?"

"That's what you wanted to say?" she asked, almost outraged.

"No." He clasped her wrist to keep her from rising. "No, but it's so incredibly beautiful, I got distracted."

"Hurry up, Jake. I need to get home. Mildred will be waiting for me."

He dared scoot just a little closer, so that he could touch her hair. "I don't think you should've flirted with all those men tonight."

She jerked her head away, swinging her hair over her shoulder. "What? That's what you wanted to say?"

"Hear me out, B.J. I mean, you shouldn't mislead them like that." He was desperately trying to find the words to tell her the revelation he'd had tonight. A revelation that shook him to the core.

A revelation he wasn't sure he could handle.

But he knew she was his woman. As much as he knew he was her man. Everyone in the entire county knew it, too.

"I don't think I was misleading anyone," she told him icily.

He leaned over and kissed her gently, briefly, unable to keep from touching her.

"Jake," she protested warningly.

"Honey, you know you were. You and I—we're perfect for each other. And we both know it. Whenever we're close to each other, the rest of the world ceases to exist. There's an attraction—hell, more like a cataclysmic explosion—when we touch. Like this." He pulled her to him and let his lips do the persuading, the convincing. As always, when he touched her, she responded like the lover he'd never had. A lover who understood his needs more than him, who was as greedy for his touch as he was for hers. A lover who would never leave him.

She opened to him, accepted him, invited him. Her hands stroked his cheeks, his chest, as his did hers. The sexy, bare shoulder he'd lusted after all night welcomed his touch when he shoved off her coat. As his mouth greedily devoured hers, he managed to bare the other shoulder, as well.

"Jake," she gasped, pulling away. "We can't do this."

"Yes, we can," he whispered, and covered her lips with his again. Hell, they not only could—they *had* to.

Since her protest disappeared in a storm of caresses, he slid one hand up that devilish slit in her costume and stroked her long leg. She ran her hands over his bare arms, caressing his muscles until he thought they'd turned to jelly.

Slanting his mouth at a different angle, he devoured her all over again. She tasted of the sweetest honey, the ambrosia of life, and he thought he'd die if he couldn't taste her over and over again.

"It's not fair," she whispered as his lips sought the secret places along her neck.

"What, baby?" he asked between kisses.

"Your toga doesn't have any buttons." She was stroking his chest through his costume, molding and shaping. "I want to touch you."

He briefly pulled away. "A toga has one advantage over jeans. It's easily removed." Pulling the garment up, he ripped it over his head and tossed it away, leaving him clad only in his briefs.

She gasped, but she didn't pull away. Instead, like a magnet, her hands returned to his chest, her gaze following her hands' movement, and she smiled in pure pleasure.

"Hey, aren't you overdressed, Cleopatra?" he murmured. He'd pulled the other shoulder free, but her breasts were still covered by the white gown.

"Mine's not as easy to get off," she protested, her gaze never leaving his body, her fingertips learning him as if she were blind.

"I hope you like what you see," he teased as he reached behind her for the zipper he'd seen earlier. In only seconds, he showed her how wrong she was about her gown. It joined his toga somewhere in the hay, followed by a strapless bra. He cupped her beautiful breasts in his hands.

And knew he wouldn't be able to control himself much longer.

As if by rote, he put his hand to his back pocket for the condom he kept in his billfold. After all, he'd preached care to his brothers for years. And once he'd realized how tempted he was by B.J., he'd made sure he was prepared.

But he wasn't prepared for wearing a toga.

Damn!

Breathing hard, he pulled back. "B.J., honey...I'm not prepared."

Her eyes, heavy with desire, opened slowly, and he almost lost control at the wanting he saw there. "What?" she asked. Without waiting for an answer, her lips headed for his again.

He couldn't refuse the invitation. Not when he ached with desire, with the need for fulfillment. Not when he thought he'd die if he didn't kiss her. Their tongues danced with hunger, stroking and pleading. Their bodies pressed against each other, as if to imprint their shapes.

Their hands reached simultaneously for the last garments they wore, but that movement reminded Jake again of his problem. "Honey, I don't have any protection. I didn't think—"

She ignored him, and his briefs joined the rest of his clothes. When her hands explored the last secrets of his body, he thought he would explode. He slipped her panties down her long legs, aided by B.J.

"Now, Jake, now, oh please," she pleaded, almost sobbing.

Jake Randall, the sane, responsible older brother, the man who'd threatened and warned his brothers against carelessness, the one who'd planned never to put his heart on the line again, plunged into her, ignoring his own warnings.

And found heaven.

B.J. KNEW SHE'D DONE something terribly wrong. But she felt so good, so complete, that she told herself she must be mistaken. The demands of the day, a long, difficult one, coupled with the events of the evening, lulled her into a delightful place where only the warm body next to her had any meaning. Only the strong arms holding her were important.

Until she woke up a few hours later.

Something had disturbed her, pulling her from sleep. She snuggled against the warmth beside her, pulling the blanket closer to her. Arms tightened satisfactorily around her, and she almost drifted off to sleep again.

Almost.

Arms? Arms around her? Warm body next to her?

Comprehension returned instantly. And with it a sick realization of what she'd done.

Because as wonderful as last night had been, and making love had taken on an entirely new meaning to B.J., she'd made a mistake.

She couldn't have an affair with Jake Randall. For

Toby's sake, she couldn't be so irresponsible. And for her sake. Because her heart would break in two.

Even now, when she knew she had to leave him, she ached with longing. She wanted to have the right to awaken him and repeat the wonder of the night. She wanted to have the right to claim him as her own.

But he'd already told her that was impossible. He had no intention of marrying.

Even if he did, she'd have to say no.

She closed her eyes, shutting out the vision of Jake Randall, his features softened in sleep, his face darkened with a heavy shadow of a beard. How she wanted to feel those stubbly cheeks, but he would awaken. She couldn't risk that.

What was she going to do now? Live next door to him and stay in the perpetual hell of wanting him?

Leave, taking Toby away from his new home, his hero worship of Jake, his second mother, Mildred? Dear God, how could she have been so irresponsible? How could she have given in to desire at the cost of her son's...and her...happiness?

The pain her actions would cause gave her the strength to slip from beneath the blanket, to hurriedly but quietly search for her clothing and run from the barn into the early-morning winter of Wyoming.

It was no colder than her heart.

JAKE STIRRED, shifted against the blanket and reached for B.J.

She wasn't there.

His eyes popped open and he sat up, letting the

blanket slide down his chest. He stared at the place she should be, but it was empty. In his mind, he traced their movement of the night before, wonder and happiness filling him as he remembered their coming together.

He'd never experienced anything like their loving. But he hoped to share it with B.J. again and again, for the rest of his life.

But where was she?

He gathered his clothes, hastily donning the toga. Before he could look for B.J., he needed to get back in his jeans, his boots. Those loose, flowing garments the Romans wore didn't do much to help a guy stay in control. No wonder the Roman Empire had collapsed.

When he stepped outside, he realized the Romans had another problem. Sandals and short dresses weren't much protection against a Wyoming winter. He hotfooted it across the snow. As he burst into the kitchen, he discovered Red already there.

Damn! He'd hoped to slip in unnoticed.

"Well, well, well. Celebrate your birthday to your satisfaction?" Red asked, a knowing grin on his face.

Jake couldn't deny that the celebration had been spectacular. But he wouldn't feel easy until he found B.J. There were some things he'd forgotten to explain to her last night.

Chapter Fifteen

B.J. had no intention of talking to anyone this morning. She had no answers to the questions crowding her head. And she didn't want to answer anyone else's questions.

She took a quick shower and dressed in her customary jeans and shirt. Folding the costume from last night, she left it lying on her bed where Mildred would find it. Her aunt could return it to the Randalls later.

As she turned to leave the room, she noticed a piece of hay clinging to the white material. Quickly she plucked it off and threw it in the trash. There was no need to advertise her foolish behavior.

She reached the front door just as Mildred came down the hall, heading for the kitchen.

"Where you going, B.J.? You're out early."

"I've got a call to make. I'll check with you later."

"I didn't hear the phone ring," Mildred called, but B.J. ignored her aunt's words and hurried to her pickup. As she was getting in, Mildred opened the front door.

"What about breakfast?"

"I'll get something later," she returned, and started up the engine. With a couple of inches of snow on the ground, she had to give it a moment to warm up. Her eyes darted from her house to the Randalls', afraid someone would try to stop her. She felt as though she were escaping from a prison.

She headed into town to grab a bite to eat. It was much too early to go to her first appointment. Besides, she needed some time to think.

What a mess she'd made of everything.

And the worst was falling in love with Jake Randall. She should've never allowed the movers to unpack their belongings once she'd met Jake. The awareness had been there even then. But she'd believed she could control it.

For nine months, they'd avoided each other, kept their distance. After all, she wasn't looking for a man. With Mildred's help, everything was fine.

But then Jake had wanted protection from matchmaking.

And he'd kissed her.

As if his touch had lit a slow-burning fuse, they'd come closer and closer to disaster. She had liked Jake. Now she craved his touch with all the desperation of an alcoholic searching for his next drink. She had admired Jake. Now she loved him until she thought her heart would break if she didn't have him.

And she couldn't.

He hadn't lied to her. He'd made his intentions clear. An affair would be welcome, a marriage would not. Last night he'd made his plans come true. She had no doubt that he'd make love to her again if she were here. They'd both shared their pleasure.

But she couldn't allow the incredible lovemaking to be repeated. It was too much. And not enough.

Which brought her to the most difficult decision she'd ever had to make. They, she and Toby, would have to leave. And she had to keep Mildred from coming with them.

The man she'd sold her practice to had written only recently to ask if she was settled in Wyoming. He had expanded the practice to the point that he was going to have to take on a partner.

She could return to her old job. Toby could rejoin his playmates. He'd gone to a little play school near their home two days a week. The place had child care most of the day, and her hours would be more those of a normal person.

They could make it.

They just wouldn't be happy.

A tear slid down her cheek.

EVERYONE WAS at the breakfast table by the time Jake got out of the shower, dressed and came into the kitchen.

"Your eggs are on the back of the stove," Red called from the table.

"Uh, I'm not hungry," Jake said, not slowing down.

"She's not there."

Red's quiet words stopped him.

"What are you talking about?"

"I saw her drive off just after you went upstairs. I guess she had an early-morning call." Red calmly continued eating. His brothers and their wives were watching the two of them. "Eat your breakfast."

Jake stood there, his hands on his hips, trying to decide what to do.

"You just get home?" Pete questioned, a grin on his face. "I'm going to have to have a talk with you about the hours you're keeping."

Jake snarled at him and turned to pick up his plate of eggs.

As if realizing taunting the tiger wouldn't be smart, they all turned their attention to their food.

Finally Anna said, "I hope you enjoyed your birthday, Jake."

"Yeah, it was the best birthday I've ever had, Anna. Thanks. You, too, Megan and Janie. And I love the saddle and the gloves." He stood and carried his plate over to the sink. The eggs he'd eaten were sitting in his stomach like leaden lumps.

He had to see B.J.

"That book B.J. gave you is incredible. Where are you going to put it?" Chad asked.

"I think I'll have a case made for it," Jake said as

he turned around. "I want to be able to look at it, but I don't want it to be damaged."

"That's a good idea. One of the hands at Ben's place does some nice wood carving. Want me to ask him if he has any ideas?" Pete asked.

"Yeah, fine. I've got to go." Without waiting for any more chatter from his family, he slipped out into the cold morning. He intended to ask Mildred about B.J.'s early-morning call. He could follow her to whatever ranch had had the emergency. She might even need his help.

No one spoke for several minutes after Jake left. Finally Megan asked, "Do you think he's all right? He seemed awfully...distracted."

Chad slipped his arm around his wife. "Yeah, he's distracted, all right. That's what happens when you ladies start messing around with our heads."

"I don't think his head is what got messed with," Red said dryly.

The ladies gasped in pretend shock, and Brett covered Anna's ears. "Please, Red, innocents are present."

Anna dug her elbow in his ribs. "So you think they, uh, made up?"

"I don't know. She sure lit out of here in a hurry this morning," Red said.

"But she would if she had an emergency call," Anna said. "That's what I do."

"Maybe you're right. But something don't feel right to me," Red insisted.

"Hey, that's the way I've been feeling for the last month," Megan protested, rubbing her large stomach. "Janie, I don't know how you managed to carry two babies around all the time."

"It was easier when I was pregnant than it is now." Then she grinned at her husband. "Except now Pete has to do part of the carrying."

The smile on Pete's face told everyone he loved toting his babies around, but he felt compelled to protest. "Man, Jake has no idea what he's getting into."

Red smiled at all of them. "Yes, he does, Pete. At long last, I think he does."

JAKE DISCOVERED Mildred had no more idea than he did about where B.J. had gone. When she led him to the table and poured him a cup of coffee, he took a sip and sat staring into space. Only Toby's arrival at the table woke him from his worrying.

"Mr. Jake! You remembered! I'm ready. I don't need no breakfast." He was already bouncing up and down in his pajamas.

Before Mildred could intervene, Jake hugged the little boy and then urged him to the table. "We cowboys don't go out in the cold without eating a good hot breakfast, Toby. And we sure don't go out in our pajamas. There's plenty of time, so eat."

Little conversation was necessary with Toby

around. He asked question after question about Jake's horse and where they would ride.

After answering what seemed a hundred questions, Jake was relieved when Mildred interrupted Toby's inquisition. "If you don't go get dressed, you won't get to ride with Mr. Jake."

The boy jumped from his seat so quickly, Jake was afraid he'd hurt himself. To Jake's surprise, however, he stopped suddenly and looked at his great-aunt. "May I be excused, Aunt Mildred?"

"Yes, Toby."

In a flash, he was out the door.

"What a great kid he is," Jake murmured.

"Yes, he is. B.J. is a good mother."

He grinned. "You're preaching to the convinced, Mildred."

"Good. It's about time."

"So when are you and Red going to tie the knot?"

Her briskness disappeared, and Mildred began fidgeting with her fork. "Red wants to get married by Thanksgiving."

"Sounds like a good time to me."

"That's in three weeks, Jake. I can't marry him till I know B.J.'s settled." She avoided looking at him, but Jake knew what she was asking.

He stood, hearing Toby coming down the hall. "Make your plans, Mildred," he said softly, "because B.J. *is* settled. She just doesn't know it yet."

He caught Toby as he leapt toward him, and together the two of them went outside.

"You mean you've never done any riding?" Jake asked when they reached the barn. He had assumed that Toby had been introduced to horseback riding the past summer. He remembered the picnic they'd had by the lake when Brett had been engaged to Sylvia, the senator's daughter.

"I rode with Mommy. She said I was too little." Toby looked worried. "Am I still too little, Mr. Jake?" He stood there in his jeans and boots, his hat cocked at the exact angle as Jake's, an anxious expression on his face.

"No, son, you're not too little. But right now I don't have a horse the right size for you. Today you'll ride with me. But I'll start looking around for a smaller horse and a saddle just your size. We may even have some left over from when we were boys."

"You mean I could use *your* little-boy saddle?" Toby said, his tone almost reverent.

"Why not? I've certainly outgrown it," Jake teased.

"That would be like I was your little boy," Toby said softly before covering his mouth with his hand.

Jake knelt down. "Would you want to be my little boy, Toby?"

The boy ducked his head. "Mommy said I can't be."

Jake's heart constricted, and he had trouble breathing. "When did Mommy say that?"

"After you bought me my hat."

Jake wanted to fold the boy into his arms, to assure

him that he'd be proud to be his daddy. But until he talked to B.J., he couldn't. After all, B.J. should be the first to know he'd decided to marry after all.

"Tell you what, today we'll just be friends. But who knows what will happen in the future. Even mommies change their minds."

B.J. DIDN'T GO HOME for lunch. She grabbed a sandwich in town and then stopped her truck by the pay phone at the gas station.

Using her calling card, she reached her old animal hospital in Kansas City. Within a few minutes, she and Dr. Brown had come to agreement on her return to Kansas City. She promised to phone him again on Monday to work out the final details.

Hanging up the phone, she got back in the truck. But she couldn't find the energy to start the engine. She'd taken the first step to solving her problems. And the sandwich she'd eaten was threatening to come back up.

How could she explain their move to Toby? How could she convince Mildred to stay and marry Red? How could she survive without at least seeing Jake?

But how could she stay and not want him?

Tears slowly seeped from her closed eyes, washing her pale cheeks.

A knock on her window surprised her. She opened her eyes to find Ben Turnbull staring at her. Rolling down her window with one hand, she dashed away her tears with the other. "Hi, Ben."

"Are you all right, B.J.?"

"Yes, of course. I—I had a difficult case this morning and I was just collecting myself."

"Want me to call Jake? He could come drive you home."

She stiffened. Already people considered her Jake's property. Toby would think Jake was going to become his daddy. "No, thanks. I've got some more calls to make. Thanks for checking on me."

Without waiting for a response, she started the engine of her truck and pulled away.

Ben frowned as he watched her drive away. Something was wrong. Digging a quarter out of his jeans pocket, he reached for the pay phone.

"Red? Is Jake around?"

"No. He rode out with the boys to the west pasture. Wanted to make sure the herd was okay after the snow."

Ben stood there, undecided.

"Anything wrong?"

"I just ran into B.J. She was sitting in her truck, crying. Said she'd had a bad case this morning."

"Crying?"

"Yeah. I asked her if she wanted me to call Jake, but she refused and drove off."

"Do you know where she was heading?"

"No. She didn't say."

"Okay. I'll tell Jake. Thanks for calling."

"Sure. Let me know if you need any help."

RED AND MILDRED WERE sitting at the table having a cup of coffee when Jake and Toby returned to the house around four.

"Huh, here we've been doing all the work, Toby, while these two just sit around," Jake teased.

"Aunt Mildred works real hard, Mr. Jake," Toby said earnestly before smiling at his great-aunt and giving her a hug. "I've been riding Mr. Jake's horse, Aunt Mildred. He's great big! And Mr Jake said he might find a horse just my size so I could ride by myself! Wouldn't that be neat?"

"Sure would, Toby, my boy," Mildred said, hugging him. "How about a cup of hot chocolate to warm you up? You're as cold as an icicle."

Toby giggled and climbed into a chair at the table. "Can Mr. Jake have some, too?"

"Sure. But he might prefer coffee. Jake?"

"Yeah, I'll take some coffee." He moved to the coffeepot and poured his own. "Have you heard from B.J. yet?"

Neither Red nor Mildred spoke, and Jake turned around in time to see them exchanging a glance. His breathing grew shallow as he stared at them. Then he said, "Toby, you'd better go wash your hands. I think Mildred is putting some cookies on the table."

Without any protest, Toby jumped down and raced for the kitchen door. He loved cookies.

"What is it?" Jake asked as soon as the swinging door closed behind the boy.

"Ben Turnbull called. He found B.J. sitting in her

truck crying at the gas station." Red's matter-of-fact delivery didn't lessen the panic Jake felt.

"Why? What was wrong? Did he offer to help her?"

"Yeah. She said she had a bad case this morning. Then she drove off. Didn't say where she was going."

Jake looked at Mildred. "Has she called you? Have you been home to check for messages?"

"I have our calls forwarded over here every day. She hasn't called once. And that's not like her." Mildred nibbled on her bottom lip, frowning, just the way B.J. did.

Jake began pacing the kitchen floor. "Why wouldn't she call if she's in trouble? Do you have any idea who her appointments were with today? I mean, it's a Saturday. Doesn't she usually come home early?"

"Jake, you know how vets are. They're just like Doc Jacoby. They go wherever and whenever they're needed." Mildred brought Toby's hot chocolate, prepared in the microwave, to the table, along with a plate of cookies. "I'm not surprised she's not home yet, but—but she doesn't usually cry."

Jake paced some more.

"Uh, Jake, Mildred and I have been talking. We know it's none of our business, but—but exactly what happened last night?"

Jake turned to stare at him, and Red hurriedly added, "It just seemed to Mildred that B.J. was acting funny from early this morning on. I mean, did the two of you have a fight?"

"No. We didn't fight. We made love." His bare-boned statement didn't begin to describe the events of the previous night, the wonder of their coming together. But Jake couldn't tell anyone about the emotions that filled him. At least, no one but B.J. He *wanted* to tell her.

If she'd just come home.

He ignored Mildred and Red and their reactions to his words. He didn't care what anyone thought. Except B.J. "Should I drive out and try to find her? Have you called around to see if she's made any of her normal stops?"

"I'll make some phone calls," Red volunteered.

As he got up to go to the phone, Mildred added, "It wouldn't do any good to drive around, Jake. She could be anywhere."

Toby came running back in, his hands extended. "See, Mr. Jake? I washed 'em good. Can I have some cookies now?"

"You bet, Toby. And Mildred's got your chocolate ready, too. Have you warmed up yet?"

"Yeah. I wasn't cold, 'cause you kept me warm. Mr. Jake put his jacket around me, Aunt Mildred. One of the cowboys said we looked just like twins," Toby bragged.

Jake sat down beside the little boy and shared a cookie or two with him. All he could think about was B.J., however, scarcely hearing Toby's ramblings.

He'd enjoyed the day spent with the child. More than even he had imagined. He'd expected to like it. He couldn't wait until his nephews were big enough to teach about ranching. But in his mind, Toby wasn't a nephew. He was his boy. His very own. Someone to pass on his legacy to.

He intended to marry B.J. And he hoped they'd have more children. But none of them would be more precious than Toby. Because he and Jake, along with B.J., all had chosen each other.

"I hear a truck," Mildred suddenly announced, cutting into Toby's tale of his adventures that day.

Jake bounded up from the table and ran to the window. "It's her. Keep Toby here." He grabbed his coat as he raced out of the kitchen.

In his head, he was carefully preparing the speech he should've made last night. It was past time to let B.J. in on his change of mind.

When he reached the truck, just after it came to a halt, he yanked open the door and pulled her into his arms. The speech could wait. He had to taste her lips again.

They weren't warm and soft, molding to his, as he'd remembered. Her lips were cold and barely moving. Jake pulled his head back to stare down at her. Her eyes were full of pain, her cheeks pale.

"What's wrong, sweetheart?"

She pulled away from him. "I have a headache." When she started toward her front door, he wrapped an arm around her, pulling her close to him.

"I can make it by myself," she protested, but her voice was weak, husky.

"No need to. I'll get you inside and fix you a cup

of coffee. After you take some aspirin, you'll be right as rain in no time.''

She didn't say anything else. When they reached the kitchen, he put her in a chair at the table and busied himself with the coffee. Over his shoulder, he noted that she'd buried her head in her hands.

As soon as he had the coffee going, he found the painkillers in a nearby shelf and grabbed a glass of water.

''Here. Take two of these.''

She did as he directed, saying nothing. He moved behind her to massage her neck and shoulders. If nothing else, it gave him an excuse to touch her, and it might relieve some of her tension.

''Don't!'' she ordered sharply, pulling away from him.

''Maybe you need to see a doctor. Do you get migraines?''

She'd lived there for almost a year, and he hadn't heard anything about migraines, but maybe she'd kept it hidden.

''No, I don't have a migraine. I just need to be left alone, Jake.''

There it was again, that defeated tone in her voice that he thought he'd heard when she got out of the truck. He began to think it didn't have anything to do with her headache. ''What's wrong, B.J.?''

''Nothing.''

''Ben said you'd been crying.''

''Ben's a big tattletale.''

He poured both of them a cup of coffee and joined

her at the table. "You told him you were crying because you had a bad case this morning."

She took a drink of coffee.

"Did you?"

"No."

"Were you crying because of last night?"

"Yes." No emotion was visible on her face or evident in her voice. Just a flat answer.

Jake sat there, unsure what to say. His planned speech didn't seem right. And yet he had to let her know how wonderful their future would be. "B.J., last night was—was incredible. I had no idea—"

"Yes, it was, wasn't it? Unfortunately we can't repeat it."

"What?"

"I told you I couldn't have an affair with you, Jake, so what I just said shouldn't come as a surprise." She stared straight ahead.

"I don't want an affair."

That remark got her attention. She stared at him, then rose from the table. "Good. Tell Mildred I'm going to take a nap."

As she reached the kitchen door, he finally got out the words he'd meant to say all along.

"I want to get married. I want to marry you, B.J."

She froze but didn't turn around. Finally, before she left the room, she uttered one word. "No."

Chapter Sixteen

B.J. reached her bedroom and grabbed for the door-knob. She wanted to shut out the world.

Unfortunately one stubborn cowboy had no intention of letting her do that. He grasped the edge of the door with one hand and her arm with the other.

"What do you mean, no?"

She swallowed and hoped that stupid sandwich was going to stay down. "No, I won't marry you."

"Why?"

Couldn't he leave her alone? Couldn't he take her answer at face value and go away? "I can't marry you."

"Look, B.J., I know I talked a lot of nonsense about not marrying again. But—last night I finally figured something out."

She didn't want to know. She wanted to cover her ears, close her eyes and hum. Anything to avoid the torture of hearing Jake's explanation.

She couldn't. Because Jake had released the door

and her arm and cupped her face, lifting it closer, nearer, within reach of his incredible lips.

He went on without any encouragement from her. "Last night, I realized I loved you. It didn't matter whether I married you or not. I would still love you. Always."

She supposed he expected her to fall into his arms. Given a choice, that would be her reaction. But she didn't have a choice. She was a mother first, and a woman second, and Toby's best interests were paramount. "No."

Shock, then irritation, crossed his face. He released her face and stepped back. "What do you mean?"

"I mean I can't marry you. Please go away." She turned her back on him. Seeing him only made her words harder to say.

Silence was her only answer. Then she heard his hard boots clumping down the hall, followed by the door slamming. He'd done as she asked.

She fell on the bed, her heart broken, tears streaming down her face.

JAKE COULDN'T BELIEVE IT. He hadn't been mistaken. Last night B.J. had shared the pleasure they'd had. She'd felt what he felt. He knew it.

But today she'd rejected him. Why? What had gone wrong?

He entered the kitchen, expectant gazes meeting his. He spoke to Mildred. "B.J. needs you. We'll keep Toby here."

"Is Mommy sick?" Toby asked, a worried frown on his face as Mildred hurried outside.

"Yeah. She has a headache. So noisy little boys need to stay here. Want to watch a video?" Jake couldn't imagine anything he'd like less, but he knew B.J. wouldn't want Toby near her right now.

He only wished she wanted *him* near her.

"You okay, boy?" Red asked.

Jake couldn't answer. His dreams had been shattered. Dreams he hadn't even realized he'd had until too late. He'd protested so much about marriage, he hadn't realized how perfect he and B.J. were for one another. Instead, he'd flaunted his refusal to marry in her face.

Was that the problem? She didn't believe him?

Hell, how could she not after last night? How could she think he could even think of another woman after holding her, loving her? How could she think he wouldn't want her at his side the rest of his life?

Because he'd told her he wouldn't.

He squared his shoulders. He wasn't going to give up. He and B.J. were meant for each other. He'd convince her. Of course he would.

"Jake?" Red repeated.

"Yeah?"

"You okay?"

Jake nodded. He couldn't bring himself to say the words, to give another lie. "Come on, Toby. Let's go watch a movie."

As he and the little boy, his hand resting in Jake's,

left the room, Jake looked at Red. "Call me if you hear anything."

Red nodded.

Over an hour later, Red called them to dinner.

Jake stared at him, a question in his eyes. Red shook his head no.

"Maybe you should call."

"She hasn't switched the phone back. I tried."

Jake opened his mouth to offer another suggestion, but Red shook his head no again. "She'll let me know, boy. We just have to be patient."

Jake explained Toby's presence by saying B.J. was letting him pretend to be a cowboy all day, including eating with his cohorts.

Toby enjoyed the teasing he received. He also liked watching the twins as they took their bottles just before dinner. Janie even let him hold each one of them briefly, hovering over him.

"They're sure little," he said. "Was I that little?"

"I imagine you were," Jake agreed.

"Did my daddy hold me?"

Jake's heart twisted. "Yeah, son, he held you. Just like I held you today."

"But you didn't feed me a bottle!" Toby said with a giggle.

"Reckon he didn't change your diaper, either," Pete added, a grin on his face.

Everyone but Jake laughed as Toby gave a disgusted look. But Jake realized he wished he'd been there for Toby's beginning. He wished he'd fathered him.

If he couldn't convince B.J. to marry him, he'd have his heart broken twice. Once by B.J., and once by the boy beside him.

Then Mildred came in.

Jake leapt to his feet.

Red got up, too, and greeted Mildred with a kiss. "Hi, sweetheart. Want some dinner?"

"Yes, that'd be fine."

Jake couldn't wait, in spite of Red's attempt to make everything look normal. "How's B.J.?"

"She's sleeping."

"Something wrong?" Anna asked.

"B.J. had a bad headache."

"Shall I go check on her?" Anna's nursing skills frequently came in handy on the ranch.

Jake held his breath. He didn't think B.J. would want Anna to come, but he was worried about her.

"No, she'll be all right. She just needed some rest," Mildred said calmly. But Jake noticed she didn't meet his gaze.

He stirred his food on his plate, but he couldn't eat anything else. He was too worried about B.J....and their future. How ironic it would be if, after helping his brothers find love, he should be the one who crashed.

Dear God, help her change her mind.

B.J. WOKE UP around eleven o'clock.

The house was dark.

With a sigh, she pushed herself up from the bed. She needed a drink of water. And maybe a hot bath. And maybe a new life.

Mildred had appeared as soon as Jake left. B.J. knew he'd sent her, that he'd told her something was wrong. But Mildred had offered a wet cloth to soothe her headache. And she'd sat beside her bed, asking no questions.

B.J. had asked only one. "Toby?"

"He's having dinner with the Randalls."

So B.J. had closed her eyes and sought relief from the pain…in her head and in her heart.

The headache had gone, she realized as she made her way to the kitchen. The pain in her heart would never go away. Because Jake was right. They were perfect for each other.

Except for one thing.

Toby.

Jake wanted Randall blood, his blood, to carry on the name, the ranch. If she married him and they had children, he would be ecstatic. And Toby would be devastated.

He'd never had a daddy, as far as he could remember. He wanted Jake in that role. It would crush him if Jake didn't think of him as his son.

She couldn't do that to her darling child.

She was an adult. She could bear the pain of loss, of separation. She'd already done it once when she lost Darrell.

Hysterical laughter bubbled up inside her. How could she compare that pale affection she'd had for Darrell to the all-consuming emotion Jake evoked?

But she'd survive. Of course she would.

Turning on the light in the kitchen, she crossed to the sink and took down a glass.

The door opened behind her.

"How are you feeling?" Mildred asked.

"Fine, thanks. I appreciate your taking care of me."

"Want to talk?"

No, she didn't want to talk. She didn't want to tell Mildred that she was leaving, she and Toby. But she had to. The longer she waited, the more difficult it would be.

"Yes, let's talk." She pulled out a chair and sat down.

After Mildred had joined her, she said, "This is hard for me to say, Mildred, but—but our move here isn't working out for me. I'm going to take Toby and move back to Kansas City."

She saw the panic and devastation in Mildred's eyes. Pain pierced her, but she couldn't let it change her mind.

Finally Mildred said, "Okay." Her voice shook.

"You're not coming with me, Mildred," B.J. said softly, hoping Mildred would accept her words.

Mildred pressed her lips tightly together. "Of course I am."

B.J. fought back the tears and reached out to clasp

Mildred's hands. "I want you to, Mildred. I don't know how I'll make it without you. Not because I can't manage, but because I love you. You've been my mother and Toby's grandmother. You've given us the love we needed."

Mildred's tears slid down her cheeks. "I love you both. We're family. Of course I'll come with you."

"No. You love Red now, too. I'd never forgive myself if I stopped you from living life to the fullest." Now B.J.'s cheeks were wet, too. "We—we'll keep in touch, write, call. Toby and I will be here for your wedding, whenever it will be." She swallowed a sob. "But I can't stay here."

"Are you sure?" Mildred pleaded.

B.J. looked away, unable to bear the pain in Mildred's gaze, and tried to smile through her tears. "I'm sure."

Before Mildred could ask her again, or ask for an explanation, B.J. rose and ran from the kitchen.

IT WAS SUNDAY. Everyone slept a little later that one day of the week, rising slowly, leisurely. Jake could imagine his brothers lingering in bed with their wives.

He hadn't been able to sleep.

Red had found him hunched over the table, a cup of coffee in his hands, when he entered the kitchen.

Now the two of them, with nothing to say, sat staring into their mugs.

Until Mildred burst into the kitchen.

Red leapt up, and she ran into his arms, tears

streaming down her face. "She's leaving," she gasped out.

Her words electrified Jake. He jumped to his feet.

And worried Red. "But you're staying?" he asked, hunger and hope in his voice.

"She won't let me go with her."

"What do you mean?" Jake demanded. "Where's she going?"

"Back to Kansas City. To her old job. She and Toby."

"When?" Jake's voice was hard, intrusive. He knew Mildred wanted to be alone with Red. But Jake had to know what B.J. had said.

"I don't know. Soon."

"Did she say why?" he asked.

Mildred shook her head.

He strode from the kitchen.

"She's still in bed," Mildred called.

He ignored her. Besides, he couldn't think of a better place for B.J. to be.

Leaping onto the porch, he was glad no one ever locked their doors. Otherwise, he'd have to break it down. Reaching into his back pocket, he pulled out his handkerchief. Without knocking, he threw open the front door and charged down the hall to B.J.'s bedroom.

When he opened this door, prepared to wake her, he discovered she was already awake, staring at the ceiling. He leaned against the wall beside the door after he shut it, afraid to go any closer. They had to get a few things straight before he could touch her.

"Jake!" she gasped, and pulled the covers to her chin.

As if he hadn't seen her gloriously naked already.

Instead of answering, he raised his white handkerchief in the air.

She frowned, a puzzled look on her face. "What?"

"Don't you recognize the universal sign of surrender?" he asked grimly.

"Surrender to what?" Her voice was tight, and she drew herself to a sitting position, leaning against the headboard.

"To whatever is keeping us apart."

Her eyes darkened, as if with pain, and she looked away. "I don't know what you're talking about."

"Yes, you do," he drawled. "I'm the one who's in the dark. I stayed up almost all night trying to figure out what went wrong."

She flashed him an angry look.

"I know I was arrogant," he admitted. Better to confess his sins than have her tell him. "Damn it, B.J., I didn't know!"

"Know what?"

"That it could be like this. That I could feel this way. With Chloe, I—I wanted her. But I didn't love her. And my wanting wasn't much. After we married, and I slept with her, I realized it was a momentary thing."

"Maybe this—this feeling will turn out to be momentary, too," she suggested, still not looking at him.

"Why won't you look at me?"

She flashed him another glare. Then looked away again.

"You know as well as I do that it's not momentary. You're as hungry for me as I am for you."

"Maybe I'm a nymphomaniac," she muttered.

"And you've kept away from men for four years?" Her suggestion was so ridiculous, it gave him hope.

"Go away, Jake."

He couldn't stay by the wall any longer. Crossing the room, he sat down on the edge of her bed. "I waved a white flag, Barbara Jo. I'll do whatever you want me to do. If you want to go back to Kansas City, then I'll go to Kansas City with you."

"Leave the ranch?" She stared at him. "Jake, the ranch is the most important thing in the world to you! That's why you found wives for your brothers. So the ranch could continue in the Randall name!"

"I want the Randall name to continue. I want the ranch to remain in the family. But that's all taken care of. You are more important to me than any piece of land."

"You'd be miserable in Kansas City," she muttered, her fingers picking at the bedspread, her gaze down.

"I'll be miserable without you wherever I am."

The tears began again, and he couldn't stand it.

"Don't cry, sweetheart," he insisted, pulling her into his arms. "We'll be happy, I promise."

Her arms held him as much as he held her, and it filled his heart with joy. "You know how I realized things were different with you? Other than the fact that I couldn't keep my hands off you? You couldn't keep your hands off me, either." He grinned and lowered his head for a kiss.

"That's why I have to leave."

He'd begun to believe he'd convinced her. Until those words.

Sobering, he said, "I think you'd better explain yourself."

Instead, she buried her head in his shirt and shook her head no.

"B.J., I love you. I want to spend the rest of my life with you. You've got to tell me what the problem is."

Finally she whispered, "Toby."

Jake frowned and pushed her back against the bed. "Toby? You think he's a problem?" His heart ached again as he considered her meaning. "He doesn't want me as a daddy?"

"Of course he wants you as a daddy," B.J. protested before a sob escaped. "But a real daddy. Not—not—"

"Not what? What are you talking about?"

"I don't want him to be second-best, Jake! I couldn't stand it!"

Completely confused, Jake shook his head. "Second-best to what?"

"Any children we might have. Any real children."

Jake sat back, stunned. Finally he said, "Dear God, B.J., is that what your refusal was for? Because you thought I couldn't love Toby as much as any other children we'd have?"

She nodded.

"I ought to pull you over my knees and paddle your behind! Except I might get distracted by your cute little rear before I got very far. Come here." He suited his actions to words, pulling her back into his embrace.

"But, Jake—" she protested, tears still falling.

"B.J., Toby and I already love each other. If you'll let me, I'll adopt him. Then he'll be a Randall in name. But he's already a Randall in my heart."

"Are you sure, Jake? He won't have your blood."

"Neither do you, sweetheart, but do you think that makes any difference about how I feel about you?"

A shining light was in her eyes, drying up her tears, and her hands slid around his neck. "Are you sure?"

"Very sure. And I'm ready to show you. How perfect that you're already in bed."

"But Toby—"

"I closed the door. And Toby has to learn that his daddy can't always be available." He covered her mouth with his and immediately felt his control slipping. She did that to him. "Especially when the distraction is his mommy."

"Oh, Jake, I was hurting so," she murmured as she surrendered to his kiss.

"Me too, Barbara Jo," he assured her huskily, "but nothing is going to come between us ever again. The three of us. We're a family, the Randall family."

She closed her eyes and hugged him tightly.

"And I'll never let you go," they both promised together.

Epilogue

Jake pulled his truck to a halt. He'd run into town to pick up some last-minute purchases B.J. insisted she needed.

Toby came flying out of the house, running in his direction, his hat sitting snugly on his head.

Jake grinned. About time for another trip to town. B.J. was right. The boy had outgrown his birthday gift in about a year. Today was only three days away from Halloween. And it was his and Toby's birthday.

Opening the door, he got out and caught Toby as he launched himself at him. If the boy got much bigger, he'd knock him over.

"Daddy! You're back."

"I am, son. How's Mom?"

"Fine. 'Cept Anna says the baby's coming."

"What?" Jake roared. He tucked Toby under one arm and ran for the house.

"Anna won't let me watch," Toby complained, his voice bouncing as much as his body.

As soon as he got inside, Jake set Toby down.

"You stay here," he ordered, and rushed up the stairs.

He entered their bedroom, finding it full of people. Mildred, Anna and Doc were around the bed. He ignored them all, falling to his knees beside B.J. "Barbara Jo, how dare you start without me."

"I knew you'd get back in time," she whispered, a smile on her beautiful lips. "But it's a good thing you didn't take any longer. This baby is getting—" She broke off to gasp as a pain seized her.

Stroking back her hair, he attempted to finish her sentence. "Impatient?"

"Yeah," she said after the pain passed.

And she was right. Within minutes, as he watched and held B.J.'s hand, his precious daughter entered the world. When her frail cry signaled her protest, he buried his face in B.J.'s hair, hiding the tears.

"Well, well, well," Doc said, a smile in his voice, "you have a baby girl, B.J. A beautiful baby girl."

"Is she all right?" B.J. asked, her eyes following Doc as he handed the baby to Anna.

Jake raised his head as Mildred, Anna and Doc all replied at once, "She's beautiful."

"Just like her mama," Jake assured everyone, a beaming smile on his face.

TWO WEEKS LATER, after he'd held his tiny daughter in his arms for the dedication service at church, Jake greeted his family and neighbors in the big living room on the Randall ranch.

"I'm not much for speech making, but as you all know, a lot of things have changed in the past couple of years."

His gaze turned to his wife, sitting in a nearby chair, holding Caroline in her arms as Toby leaned against the chair. "Two years ago, we were a bunch of bachelors living a pretty dull existence. Everyone teased me about my matchmaking, but it was the smartest thing I've ever done."

"Here, here!" Chad called, drawing laughter from the group.

"Now B.J. and I have been blessed, not only with the love we share, but also with two wonderful children. Janie and Pete have their twins, Chad and Megan have Elizabeth. Only Brett and Anna haven't— Yes, Brett?"

Brett had waved a hand at his brother, halting his speech. "Actually that's not true, Jake. Anna and I are expecting our own Randall in about seven months."

Anna's cheeks turned bright pink amid all the congratulations. B.J. reached out and squeezed her hand, and Janie and Megan came over to kiss her cheek.

"Hey, how about me?" Brett protested. "I had something to do with this baby, too." The Randall women laughed and kissed his cheek.

"Well, it looks like we're celebrating more than Caroline. I guess that only leaves Mildred and Red. Got an announcement for us, Red?" Everyone broke into delighted laughter, and Mildred chastised Jake for his teasing.

Red, however, spoke up. "Me and Mildred will take care of the grandparenting, boy. You young ones just keep producing them."

"Yeah," Toby spoke up. "Next time we want a boy so I can have a brother."

"Next time?" B.J. asked faintly, but Jake heard her. He smiled, his heart full. In spite of her protest, he knew she'd welcome as many more children as God blessed them with.

Ben Turnbull called out, "Yeah, next time, B.J. You know how important it is to keep the Randall line going."

Jake nodded at his friend. "Yeah, I always thought keeping the Randall line going was important. But I've discovered something more important." He paused and smiled at his wife again. "I've discovered that the most important thing in the world is love. Love between friends, love between brothers, love between a father and his children—" he smiled specially at Toby, who glowed "—and most of all, love between a man and his wife."

He lifted his glass. "Here's to the happiness we've found."

Bending down, he briefly kissed B.J., Toby and Caroline, then raised his glass again before taking a deep, long drink, as his brothers did.

The Randalls had a lot to celebrate.

You asked for it....You got it! More MEN!

We're thrilled to bring you another special edition of the wildly popular MORE THAN MEN series.

Like those who have come before him, Mitch Rollins is more than tall, dark and handsome. All of these men have extraordinary powers that make them "more than men." But whether they're able to grant you three wishes or live forever, make no mistake—their greatest, most extraordinary power is that of seduction....

So make a date with Mitch in...

JUST ONE TOUCH
by Mary Anne Wilson

It's a date you'll never forget!

Available in March wherever Harlequin books are sold.

Take 4 bestselling love stories FREE

Plus get a FREE surprise gift!

THIRTY.

    SINGLE.

        ON A HUSBAND HUNT.

Clarissa, Maggie and Hallie have their practical reasons for attempting to override fate. And they're not leaving anything to chance!

> - They selected eligible bachelors.
> - Did their research.
> - Consulted their lists and spreadsheets, their bar graphs and flow charts—even double-checked with a wizened soothsayer, just to be sure— before they narrowed it down to:
>
> √ a <u>millionaire</u>   √ a <u>cowboy</u>   √ <u>the boy next door</u>

But will a roguish millionaire, a genuine Texas cowboy and the boy next door show these little ladies that you just can't forgo passion for tidy emotions?

How To Marry...

A MILLION-DOLLAR MAN
Vivian Leiber
(March)

ONE HOT COWBOY
Cathy Gillen Thacker
(April)

THE BAD BOY NEXT DOOR
Mindy Neff
(May)

HARLEQUIN®

Don't miss these Harlequin favorites by some of our most distinguished authors!
And now, you can receive a discount by ordering two or more titles!

HT#25645	THREE GROOMS AND A WIFE by JoAnn Ross	$3.25 U.S. $3.75 CAN.	☐
HT#25647	NOT THIS GUY by Glenda Sanders	$3.25 U.S. $3.75 CAN.	☐
HP#11725	THE WRONG KIND OF WIFE by Roberta Leigh	$3.25 U.S. $3.75 CAN.	☐
HP#11755	TIGER EYES by Robyn Donald	$3.25 U.S. $3.75 CAN.	☐
HR#03416	A WIFE IN WAITING by Jessica Steele	$3.25 U.S. $3.75 CAN.	☐
HR#03419	KIT AND THE COWBOY by Rebecca Winters	$3.25 U.S. $3.75 CAN.	☐
HS#70622	KIM & THE COWBOY by Margot Dalton	$3.50 U.S. $3.99 CAN.	☐
HS#70642	MONDAY'S CHILD by Janice Kaiser	$3.75 U.S. $4.25 CAN.	☐
HI#22342	BABY VS. THE BAR by M.J. Rodgers	$3.50 U.S. $3.99 CAN.	☐
HI#22382	SEE ME IN YOUR DREAMS by Patricia Rosemoor	$3.75 U.S. $4.25 CAN.	☐
HAR#16538	KISSED BY THE SEA by Rebecca Flanders	$3.50 U.S. $3.99 CAN.	☐
HAR#16603	MOMMY ON BOARD by Muriel Jensen	$3.50 U.S. $3.99 CAN.	☐
HH#28885	DESERT ROGUE by Erine Yorke	$4.50 U.S. $4.99 CAN.	☐
HH#28911	THE NORMAN'S HEART by Margaret Moore	$4.50 U.S. $4.99 CAN.	☐

(limited quantities available on certain titles)

	AMOUNT	$
DEDUCT:	10% DISCOUNT FOR 2+ BOOKS	$
ADD:	POSTAGE & HANDLING	$
	($1.00 for one book, 50¢ for each additional)	
	APPLICABLE TAXES*	$_____
	TOTAL PAYABLE	$_____
	(check or money order—please do not send cash)	

To order, complete this form and send it, along with a check or money order for the total above, payable to Harlequin Books, to: **In the U.S.:** 3010 Walden Avenue, P.O. Box 9047, Buffalo, NY 14269-9047; **In Canada:** P.O. Box 613, Fort Erie, Ontario, L2A 5X3.

Name: _____

Address: _____ City: _____

State/Prov.: _____ Zip/Postal Code: _____

*New York residents remit applicable sales taxes.
 Canadian residents remit applicable GST and provincial taxes.
Look us up on-line at: http://www.romance.net

HBACK-JM4

FREE VALENTINE'S BROOCH! $9.95 U.S. retail value

This Valentine's Day Harlequin brings you all the essentials—romance, chocolate and jewelry—in:

VALENTINE *Delights*

Matchmaking chocolate-shop owner Papa Valentine dispenses sinful desserts, mouth-watering chocolates...and advice to the lovelorn, in this collection of three delightfully romantic stories by Meryl Sawyer, Kate Hoffmann and Gina Wilkins.

As our special Valentine's Day gift to you, each copy of *Valentine Delights* will have a beautiful, filigreed, heart-shaped brooch attached to the cover.

Make this your most delicious Valentine's Day ever with *Valentine Delights!*

Available in February wherever Harlequin books are sold.

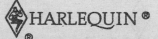
HARLEQUIN ®

Look us up on-line at: http://www.romance.net   VAL97

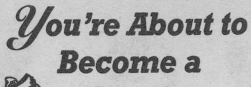